DEVIL'S
PASS

SIGMUND BROUWER

DEVIL'S PASS

ORCA BOOK PUBLISHERS

Library and Archives Canada Cataloguing in Publication

Brouwer, Sigmund, 1959-
Devil's pass / Sigmund Brouwer.
(Seven (the series))

Issued also in an electronic format.
ISBN 978-1-55469-938-4

I. Title. II. Series: Seven the series
PS8553.R68467D47 2012   jc813'.54   C2012-902582-8

First published in the United States, 2012
Library of Congress Control Number: 2012938220

Summary: Webb, a young street musician, faces grizzly bears and a madman
on the Canol Trail when he tries to fulfill a request in his late grandfather's will.

MIX
Paper from
responsible sources
FSC® C016245

*Orca Book Publishers is dedicated to preserving the environment and has printed
this book on paper certified by the Forest Stewardship Council®.*

Orca Book Publishers gratefully acknowledges the support for its publishing
programs provided by the following agencies: the Government of Canada
through the Canada Book Fund and the Canada Council for the Arts,
and the Province of British Columbia through the BC Arts Council
and the Book Publishing Tax Credit.

Design by Teresa Bubela
Cover photography by Terry Parker
Author photo by Reba Baskett
Lyrics to "Monsters" courtesy of Drew Ramsey/Cindy Morgan/Chris Wild,
Green Bike Music (ASCAP)

ORCA BOOK PUBLISHERS
PO Box 5626, Stn. B
Victoria, BC Canada
V8R 6S4

ORCA BOOK PUBLISHERS
PO Box 468
Custer, WA USA
98240-0468

www.orcabook.com
Printed and bound in Canada.

15 14 13 12 • 4 3 2 1

First, to Alasdair Veitch: You are a great trail guide, an amazing biologist and one of the few who has walked every step of the Canol Trail—thanks for your help with the story. And to Michael Duclos, the principal at Mackenzie Mountain School in Norman Wells, and to the students there too—thanks for making me feel at home in the Arctic.

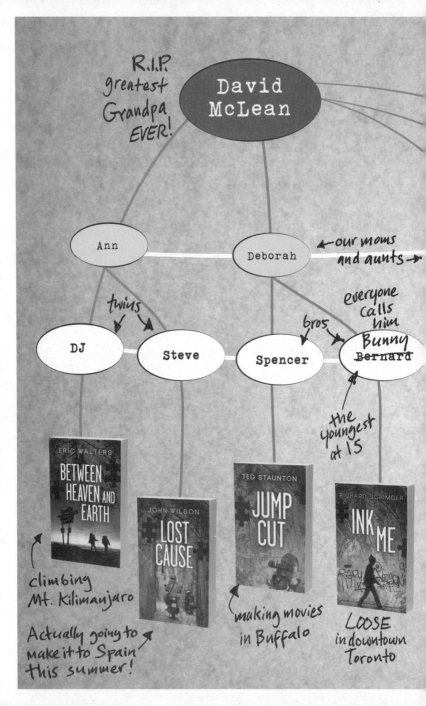

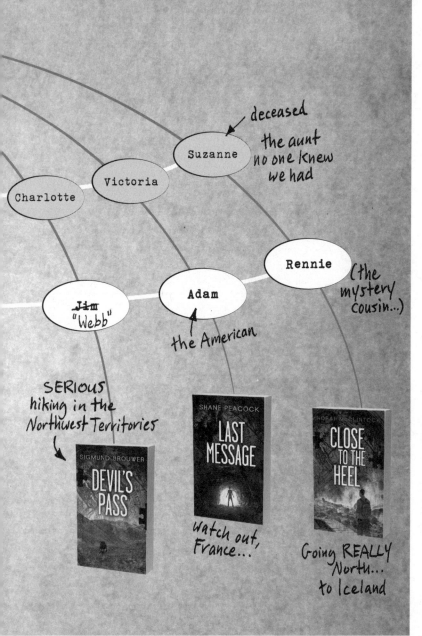

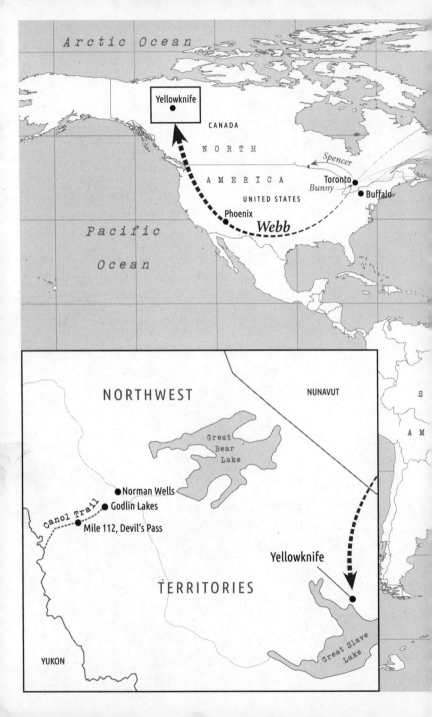

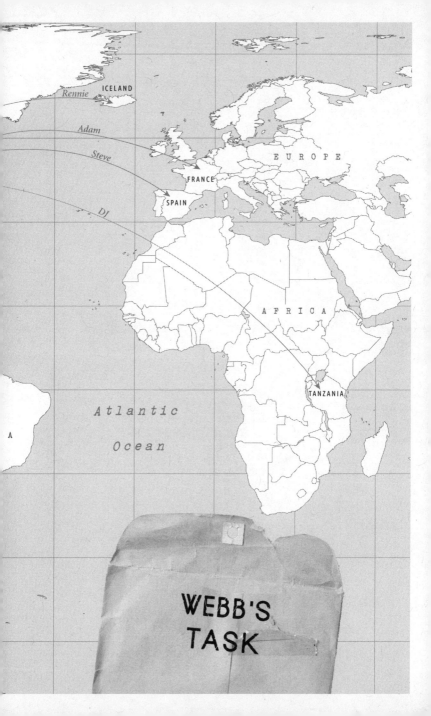

PART
ONE

THIS IS NO PICNIC

Working and living conditions on this job are as difficult as those encountered on any construction job ever done in the United States or foreign Territory. Men hired for this job will be required to work and live under the most extreme conditions imaginable. Temperature will range from 90 degrees above zero to 70 degrees below zero. Men will have to fight swamps, rivers, ice and cold. Mosquitos, flies and gnats will not only be annoying, but will cause bodily harm. If you are not prepared to work under these and similar conditions, **DO NOT APPLY**.

(On a sign from the construction company building the Canol Trail, 1942.)

ONE

NOW

Beneath the vintage black Rolling Stones T-shirt he had found at a thrift store, Webb was wearing a money belt stuffed with $2,000 in prepaid bank cards. It was a lot of money for a seventeen-year-old who worked nights as a dishwasher. The belt cut into his skin as he sat against a building on a sidewalk in downtown Yellowknife, but Jim Webb didn't feel the pain.

Not with a Gibson J-45 acoustic guitar in his hands and a mournful riff pouring from his soul as he played "House of the Rising Sun," humming along to the words in his head. Webb was killing time before he had to catch a cab out to the airport.

Playing a guitar in a hotel room drew loud, angry knocks on the wall from the other guests, but playing on the street drew cash. That was one reason for the acoustic guitar—it was uncomplicated. Electric guitars needed amps and cords. The other reason was the sound. Just Webb and his guitar and his voice. What people heard was all up to him, and there was a purity in that kind of responsibility that gave him satisfaction.

Already half a dozen people had stopped to give him the small half-friendly smiles that he saw all the time—smiles that asked, "If you're that good, why are you sitting on a sidewalk with an open guitar case in front of you, waiting for money to be tossed in your direction like you're a monkey dancing at the end of a chain?"

Those looks never bothered him. Nothing bothered him when he had a guitar in his hands. For Webb, there was no rush like it. Playing guitar, hearing guitar, feeling the strings against the calluses on his fingers and thumb, watching people watch him as he played. All of it. No other way to describe it except as the coolest feeling in the world. Instead it was how he felt when the guitar was back in the case that worried him.

This was why he wasn't napping in the hotel half a block away, where he'd been forced to stay when yesterday's flight to Norman Wells had been grounded by thick fog.

Besides, Webb didn't want to get used to comfort. At the end of the trip, he fully expected to be back in Toronto, where he needed every bit of change that found its way to the bottom of his guitar case. Washing dishes until 3:00 AM at minimum wage wasn't enough to keep him from starving.

For now, he was happy. Yesterday's fog had cleared. The midday sun was bright, and heat radiated from the concrete, adding a sense of well-being to the joy he took in playing the chords in perfect tempo and perfect rhythm. He had the guitar strung with a combo of steel strings and nylon. Not a lot of musicians did it this way, but there was a subtleness to the variation in sound that gave Webb a lot of satisfaction.

A middle-aged man with a face gray from too much booze and not enough sun wandered down the sidewalk and stopped to join the small crowd. He looked at Webb with amazement.

This wasn't a "Can you be as good as I think you are?" look. No, it was a look that Webb knew, a look that said, "I haven't seen you here before and what are doing in my territory?"

It was obvious to Webb that the man wasn't one of the herd of life's mortgage holders. Living on the streets put unmistakable grime into every stitch of what you wore because it was all you wore, all the time. Unmistakable by look and unmistakable by odor. Street bums were the same everywhere. But then, so were all the suits Webb saw in Toronto every day. The man's face wrinkled into a grin, showing broken teeth. He had lumpy ears, probably from nights spent outside in the winter, drunk. His ears must have frozen at least a couple of times. Webb had seen that before, and how grown men cried out as their ears began to thaw.

The man sat beside Webb along the wall. Like they were already street buddies. The man lifted his hands and whirled them in time with the music, as if he were the conductor responsible for Webb's dexterity.

Webb smelled the booze and figured that was what made the man so chummy. It didn't bother Webb. People did what they had to do to get by. Besides, the guy looked like he panhandled plenty, and he could have told Webb to move out of his territory.

That had happened a lot in Toronto. Webb had lived on the streets for a while too, before realizing that between a dishwashing job at night and playing music on the streets during the day he could make just enough money to live in a room at a boardinghouse.

People in front of them frowned because the street bum was a distraction. They wanted the music.

Webb eased the riff down some. Didn't want the guitar to drown out the vocals as he began to sing.

Oh, Mother, tell your children
Not to do what I have done.
Spend your lives in sin and misery
In the house of the rising sun.

Webb liked the Rolling Stones' version of "House of the Rising Sun" better than the Animals' version, even though the Animals' version was the famous one. He liked both of them better than Dylan's version. Sure, people might wonder how and why a seventeen-year-old knew about stuff like this, knew that "House of the Rising Sun" was a ballad a couple hundred years old. But all that mattered to Webb was playing a chord in the third chorus exactly the way Keith Richards had done it. He didn't care if people thought he was weird for caring about how blues had evolved into rock and roll. One of his dreams was to someday record his own version of this song.

Webb had his eyes closed as he finished. He felt a shadow across his face and looked up to see a very, very attractive woman leaning over to drop a twenty in his guitar case.

Very, very attractive. Really hot, in fact.

Brunette hair, shoulder length. Great smile. Jeans and a form-fitting hoodie. College-aged, but not the college type. Someone he'd never have a chance with.

He'd seen her the day before at the Edmonton airport, boarding his Canadian North flight a few people ahead of him in line. It was a flight with a stopover in Yellowknife on the way to Norman Wells; from there it would go on to Inuvik, just south of the Arctic Ocean. He'd seen her getting off the plane in Yellowknife and had walked behind her on the runway, the massive engines of the jets winding down into silence.

He'd seen her in line at the counter, rebooking her next flight to Norman Wells as he waited to do the same thing, all of them learning that because the fog was even worse in Norman Wells, they'd have to wait until the next day to fly. Canadian North had helped book hotel rooms for everyone in downtown Yellowknife, a ten-minute shuttle ride away. The hot woman had been at the front and Webb at the back. She'd been in line ahead of him in the hotel lobby too, checking in for the overnight stay.

He didn't remember her just because she was very, very attractive. It was because he'd noticed the trace of a bruise on her cheekbone. The bruise, which reached up almost to her left eye, looked old, but her makeup couldn't quite hide it.

The bruise had made him hyperaware of the guy who had stood close beside her everywhere: in line in Edmonton boarding the plane, in Yellowknife at the ticket counter, in the hotel lobby the day before. A black-haired guy with broad shoulders and big hands, in jeans and a jacket with the name of an oil company on it. He vibrated with animal awareness and aggression and looked to be a few years older than the woman. Webb knew about those kinds of guys too. If you didn't watch for them, you didn't survive long on the streets.

Webb was only seventeen, but his time on his own made him feel a lot older.

That's why he knew that when the woman floated a twenty-dollar bill into his guitar case, there was going to be trouble.

TWO

Webb guessed that the girl had not been with the guy for very long. Otherwise she would have known better than to show appreciation for anything another guy was doing, even if that other guy was a scruffy seventeen-year-old in a ratty Rolling Stones T-shirt.

Guys like her boyfriend didn't like any kind of competition, and guys like her boyfriend generally didn't like skinny musician types like Webb, whose hair was long enough to pull back in a ponytail.

She smiled at Webb. "That was cool," she said. "Thanks."

Webb kept his head down.

He wondered who the target would be: him or the drunk beside him. The drunk was a better bet. Much better—from the black-haired guy's view—to pick on a drunk rather than a kid.

Webb thought of hitting the guitar strings hard, ripping into a wicked set of chords he'd come up with in a park in Toronto. Sure, a successful distraction would save him or the drunk, but someone would still have to pay. Someone very, very attractive.

So he remained silent and stared at the twenty-dollar bill as if it was a stick of dynamite in his open guitar case.

The drunk broke the silence.

"Hey," he said, pointing at the twenty. "I should be a rock star too. Money and hot chicks."

Inside, Webb groaned. The street bum had lit the fuse.

Webb leaned forward and set his guitar in the case. Normally, he'd empty the change out first. He hated the thought of anything scratching his Gibson. But he wanted it in the case before he stood.

Webb made it to his feet as the black-haired guy reached down and yanked the homeless guy up by his collar. Webb kicked the lid closed and shoved the case down the sidewalk with his foot.

By then, the big black-haired guy had pushed the street bum up against the wall.

"Look, you piece of dog crap," the black-haired guy hissed, "nobody talks about my girlfriend like that."

The woman rushed up and put a hand on her boyfriend's shoulder. "Brent."

He whirled on her, and the look in his eyes was something Webb was familiar with. Not that a person ever gets used to a look like that.

"Shut up, Stephanie."

"Hey!" Webb said, drawing the guy's attention. A quick image hit him. A matador, waving a red cape at a dangerous bull. "The guy's drunk. He barely has a clue what's happening."

"You shut up too," Brent said. His tone said more than the words. Like he'd been hoping for an excuse to turn on Webb.

"Sure," Webb said, raising his hands, palms up. "No problem." A new image hit him: a dog showing its belly so that a bigger dog would leave it alone.

Webb looked over his shoulder at the people who'd been happy to listen to him busking. They were drifting away, uncomfortable and helpless.

"We're all good, right?" Webb said to Brent. "This dude's going to apologize, right?"

The street bum nodded. "Yeah, man. Didn't mean no harm."

Webb hoped it was enough to calm Brent down.

"All right then," Brent said. "Next time I won't be so nice about it."

Brent put his arm around his girlfriend and walked her away.

Webb didn't feel much like playing anymore. He opened the guitar case and took out the guitar, checking the bottom of it for scratches, hoping he hadn't been too quick putting it in the case.

The guitar was good.

And there was the twenty, along with a handful of change.

He scooped it all up. The street bum was still there, a confused smile on his face.

"You hungry?" Webb asked as he put the Gibson back in the case.

"Always."

Webb didn't give the street bum the money. That would be like putting another bottle in his hands.

"Come with me," Webb said. "I'll buy you a burger somewhere."

THREE

In the air, as the Canadian North flight descended into Norman Wells, Webb felt calm and peaceful. Something about the vastness of the unbroken expanse of green trees below had given him a sense that there were still things so big that humans couldn't reach out and spoil them.

Webb had to wait for most of the passengers to leave the airplane, because he'd taken his guitar on board, and he needed the flight attendant to get it from wherever she'd stored it during the flight.

He had the case strapped on his back as he walked down the steps of the big jet. Norman Wells had

a small airport, and airplanes here didn't pull up to
a jet bridge connected to a terminal.

Webb enjoyed the feeling of sunshine on his face
and was glad this wasn't the middle of the winter.
He couldn't imagine what it would have been like to
walk across the runway if it was minus forty with
a howling wind.

As he stepped into the airport, a man walked
toward Webb, giving him a small smile.

"You must be Jim Webb," the man said, extending
his hand. "I'm George."

Webb had expected someone to meet him.

"I'm Webb." Webb accepted the handshake.
"Nice to meet you."

George was barely taller than Webb, with dark
hair streaked with gray. He was about the age Webb's
father would have been, if he'd lived. One of the
letters in Webb's pocket had mentioned that George
was Sahtu Dene, one of the First Nations of this area
of the Northwest Arctic.

"Jim Webb. Named after the songwriter?" George
asked.

Webb was impressed. The other Jim Webb had
won Grammy Awards and had written for artists

like Elvis Presley and Frank Sinatra. A song by the other Jim Webb—"By the Time I Get to Phoenix"— was the third-most-performed song between 1940 and 1990. Webb knew this because he had learned it from his dad, a man who had loved music, who had been happy to give Webb a first name with such heritage. He had been the one to teach Webb to play guitar as soon as Webb's fingers were big enough to put pressure on the frets.

"Yes, I was named after Jimmy Webb," Webb said. "Not a lot of people know about him."

"Your dad must love music. Like me."

No point bringing the mood down and telling George that Webb's dad was dead. Or that the guitar Webb carried was not the Gibson J-45 that his dad had given him.

George pointed to the guitar case strapped on Webb's back. "Much as we both love music, you'd better want to carry that really bad. We don't leave anything on the trail. Ever. If we can't burn it, we carry it out. That applies to garbage. And guitars."

"It's coming with me," Webb said. "I've got it wrapped in plastic inside the case. It won't get wet if it rains."

George nodded.

Webb liked the fact that George didn't say something like "Are you sure?" Webb hated being treated like a child.

"Maybe then," George said, "you could find room in your case for some extra rope. Never hurts, you know, to have extra rope."

It was Webb's turn to nod, and George grunted with satisfaction.

Webb also liked that George spoke quietly, like a man who didn't have anything to prove to anybody. Webb liked that George's hands were scarred and leathery and that a couple of his fingers were bent and twisted. Hands that had been outdoors a lot, which probably meant that George had learned to survive in the wilderness. That was a good quality in a man who was going to guide Webb through desolate mountain ranges.

George followed Webb to the luggage area where Webb caught sight of Stephanie and Brent. The peace that Webb felt from being in the serenity of the Northwest Territories dropped away as surely as the plane had dropped to earth. When Webb saw that Stephanie had a new welt across her face, it hit him like the sudden jarring of wheels on a scorching runway.

Webb saw Brent duck into the washroom, leaving his girlfriend standing alone as the luggage belt lurched into motion.

It was a small airport with big windows that let in a lot of light. That should have made Webb feel cheerful, but it didn't. Because it was a small airport, he'd only have a minute with her, if he was lucky.

"George," Webb said, "can you excuse me for a minute?"

George nodded.

Webb moved to stand beside her, pretending he was just another passenger, staring at the luggage belt as if concentrating would bring the suitcases out quicker.

"It won't get better," Webb said to her. "No matter what you think."

Stephanie glanced at him like she was surprised to see him, although he was sure she knew he had been on the same plane. She had done a good job of ignoring him at the Yellowknife airport after all the passengers had cleared security, and before they'd left the terminal for the airplane.

"I don't know what you're talking about," she said. But he knew it was a lie as soon as she lifted her hand to her face.

"People don't change," Webb said. "If you stay, he'll keep hitting you. You don't deserve it. Nobody deserves it. He's not going to stop. Trust me. I know about these things."

"You can't talk to me like that," Stephanie said. "You don't know me. Or my life."

"I know all about getting pushed around though. So, yes, I can talk to you like that."

"No," she said. She gave the word a lot of emphasis.

It took Webb a fraction of second to realize she wasn't talking to him but past him. Over his shoulder. Her eyes were widening, and Webb figured out what was happening just as a huge hand grabbed his shoulder, spinning Webb away from her and toward the person she was speaking to.

Brent.

Brent's fist was already in motion. A big, big fist, filling Webb's vision as it accelerated toward his face.

No way did Webb have time to lift his arms in defense. Instead, he let himself fall backward, going with the motion of that big, big fist. He didn't even try to stay on his feet.

Going with the punch took away some of the impact but not close to enough. There was a *flash-bang* as the fist hit his face, and Webb flailed with his arms to break his fall. He also allowed his body to turn naturally with the force of the blow. Landing on his back would have been disastrous. People died that way, when their bodies hit the ground and their skulls whiplashed into the floor a fraction of a second later.

He fell onto the luggage belt, but that didn't give him any safety.

A second later, Brent hauled him up again, like Webb was a runaway suitcase.

Brent was a fast learner.

This time, as he raised his elbow to throw an overhead punch, he kept a grip on Webb's shoulder with his other hand, so that Webb wouldn't bounce away from him again.

What he didn't know was that Webb was a fast learner too. Or that Webb had done some intense martial-arts training and had lived on the streets. This wasn't Webb's first fight.

Brent had landed the first punch because Webb had had his back to him, too worried about Stephanie to focus on anything else. This time Webb saw the punch coming, telegraphed by the way Brent had drawn back his right elbow.

Again Webb went with the natural flow and didn't give Brent any resistance. Webb let Brent's left hand draw him in, and then he ducked the punch by slamming the top of his forehead into Brent's nose.

Not painful, if you do a headbutt right. The skull is an amazingly solid object.

But painful to your opponent. Because the skull is an amazingly solid object.

There was a crunch of cartilage, and Webb knew instantly he'd shattered Brent's nose. As Brent brought his hands up to the mess Webb had just made of his face, it left his lower body open.

The knee is an amazingly solid object too. Much more solid than the part of Brent's body that Webb slammed his knee into.

Brent fell to his knees, clutching his crotch, and barfed. Then he toppled into his own barf.

That's when the cop stepped into the luggage area and saw Webb standing above Brent, ready to kick him if he tried something else.

The cop barked at Webb to step away, like Webb had started the fight.

Webb looked around, hoping Stephanie would say something. Something like Brent threw the first punch.

But she was gone.

Webb looked at George. "Tell him," Webb said. "The guy threw the first punch."

"What I saw," George said, "was you walking up to the guy and hitting him without warning."

Then George folded his arms across his body.

That's why, on a sunny June afternoon three days after the reading of his grandfather's will, Webb found himself in handcuffs in the back of a cop truck outside Norman Wells airport, ninety miles south of the Arctic Circle.

FOUR

As the cop drove Webb through Norman Wells, Webb saw streets with names like Raven and Lynx. He knew from Internet research that there was also one named Honeybucket, because, in the past, that's what they called the pails they used on long frozen nights when a person didn't want to go to the outhouse.

He wasn't in the mood for sightseeing though. He was mad at himself for not paying attention in the airport. On the streets, that kind of carelessness could get a person killed.

He was also mad at George, who lived in this small town. George knew the cop who had arrested Webb.

Webb wouldn't be sitting in the cop truck if George had told the truth. No, Brent would be in it instead. But George had lied.

It didn't help Webb's mood that his lower jaw hurt. A lot. There was a tooth loose. It felt like it was sticking through his skin. He used his tongue to push his lower lip forward and touch the tooth. It was leaning forward at more than forty-five degrees. The pain felt like lightning going through his veins. But that slight touch was enough to pop the tooth loose.

With his hands cuffed behind him, there wasn't much else to do with the tooth except spit it out, swallow it or roll it under his tongue. He decided not to give the cop the satisfaction of seeing a tooth come out like a Chiclet, and he sure didn't want that small, hard chunk of enamel going through his digestive system. So he kept it under his tongue and watched the streets of Norman Wells go by.

He had never been to Norman Wells before, but he knew as much about it as a person could learn through Wikipedia. Webb disliked going anywhere without knowing what to expect. He knew every free Wi-Fi spot in a twenty-block radius of his territory in Toronto, and Google and his iPod were his best friends.

Much as it had hurt to draw from his tiny savings, he had even invested in a solar-powered battery charger so he wouldn't have to depend on coffee shops and the library for power.

Webb knew a lot about Norman Wells, but he hadn't known that the cops drove police trucks, not police cars. White with horizontal stripes like a regular police car. Same Plexiglas and bars between the front seat and the back, but in a 4x4. Made sense, given the climate.

The cop pulled up to a building on a corner across a gravel parking lot from a fenced playground. Symbolic, Webb thought. Ironic, even. A playground for those who still had lots of opportunity to make good choices; police station for those who hadn't. Probably lost on people who spent time in the police station, but not lost on him. Maybe a song was in there somewhere, he thought, losing himself in that instead of worrying about what lay ahead. That's what he always did—escaped into the music. Most of the time it worked. Now his anger and the broken tooth were distractions.

The cop hit a button on a remote on the visor, and the door to a huge garage bay opened. The cop slowly drove the truck into the garage and shut the door with the remote before opening the rear passenger door of the police truck.

"I'm going to escort you up the steps and inside to your holding cell," the cop said. "And by escort, that means you'll walk in front of me and I'll be watching to make sure you keep walking and don't try anything stupid."

Webb poked at the new hole in his mouth, where a healthy tooth had been less than a half hour earlier. Good that he'd had lots of experience dealing with pain, he thought.

"Did you hear that?" the cop said. "Do me a favor and don't try anything stupid."

Webb's hands were cuffed behind his back, so trying anything at all would by definition be trying something stupid. Must have been plenty before him who had been stupid, if it needed saying.

"Come on," the cop grunted. "Let's get this done."

Webb swung his legs out of the truck, then paused.

"My guitar," Webb said. The cop had thrown the case in the back of the truck. Thrown. That was the real crime here. "Can you put it somewhere safe?"

"Yeah, yeah," the cop said. "Somewhere safe."

No way Webb would have been able to afford the guitar on his own. His grandfather had co-signed a loan for it. It was the only time Webb had asked anyone for help since he left home. He was making weekly payments, but it was worth the cost, both in money and in asking for a favor. The J-45 was legendary. Its rosette—the circle around the sound hole—was three-ply binding, something that probably only someone like Webb could love and appreciate. The teardrop-shaped pick guard was polished tortoise. A top of Sitka spruce and sides of Honduras mahogany gave it the warm bass sound and amazing projection that plucked at your soul.

Webb wanted to ask the cop not to toss it around while he was finding somewhere safe, but he didn't want to annoy the cop and have him do the opposite.

On his feet, Webb found his balance, and the cop used a hand on the small of Webb's back to push him forward, up a set of steps, through a security door and into the police station.

Not much to see. Three numbered doors, all of them open. Webb glanced inside as the cop pushed him past the doors toward a counter. The interiors of the rooms were bare, with bench seats around all the walls. Toilet in the corners. Cells. The rooms were cells.

One of them, Webb guessed, would be his new home.

At the counter, the space opened up into a public lobby. There were a couple of desks with computers. Not much else.

Webb had no idea whether this was a typical police station. This was a first for him.

"Want to know what happens next?" the cop asked. Like he had read Webb's mind. Or like he was curious about why Webb looked as if he didn't care. Webb had a lot of practice looking like he didn't care.

"Can I do anything about it if there's something I don't like?"

"Nope."

"Any chance I can have my guitar back while I wait for whatever happens next?"

"Nope."

"Then go ahead with whatever happens next. I don't see much point in getting it explained to me."

"Somehow, I'm not surprised," the cop said. "I'm going to need your belt and everything in your pockets. Once you're in the cell, I'll see if I can get a nurse to come in and look at your lip. The doctor's not scheduled to be here until next week."

"How about you let me out of here," Webb said. "I didn't do anything wrong except defend myself."

"Your tooth went right through your lip," the cop said. "Someone should look at it."

"I'd rather see a lawyer. I need to get out of here."

"Lawyer?" The cop laughed. "Here in Norman Wells? You did notice how isolated we are, right?"

"I've noticed you have telephones," Webb said. "Let me call a lawyer."

"Any particular reason?"

"Yes." But that's all Webb said.

"That would be?"

That would be something that his grandfather had asked Webb to do, but it would also be something that was none of the cop's business.

Webb said nothing. He'd learned silence was a powerful way to communicate.

The cop let out a long sigh. Webb could tell he was puzzled. But Webb didn't owe him any explanations.

"What brings you to Norman Wells?" the cop asked.

"Airplane," Webb said.

"From anyone else," the cop said, "that would be a smart-ass answer. You, I think, are telling me to mind my own business. But after what you did at the airport, your business is my business."

Webb took off his belt and emptied out his pockets. Some change. His wallet. A few guitar picks. His iPod and the solar-powered charger.

"You're forgetting something."

Webb shook his head.

"That tooth. If it's not attached to you, it goes in the bag too."

"Swallowed it," Webb said. He felt the tooth roll under his tongue as he spoke.

After he filled in a form listing all Webb's belongings, the cop chucked all Webb's stuff in a bag and uncuffed Webb so that he could sign the form. Webb could see the cop watching him, as if he expected Webb to swing at him and wanted to be ready for it.

No chance of that. The cop had control of the guitar. Webb didn't want the cop to have a personal grudge against him. Webb could fight back. His guitar couldn't.

"Give me your parents' phone number," the cop said as he flipped through Webb's passport. "You're not eighteen."

Webb couldn't imagine anything worse—after ignoring his mother at the funeral and the reading of the will, his first contact with her in months shouldn't be a call from a police cell in the Northwest Territories. She didn't deserve that.

"I have to be out by tomorrow," Webb said. "Don't I get a phone call or something?"

"I want to talk to your parents."

"And I want to talk to a lawyer."

"Tomorrow," the cop said. He led Webb to cell number two. "And if you don't give me a number for your parents, I'll get it another way. Trust me."

The benches along the walls were green. There were two large windows made of some kind of material that let in light but wasn't transparent.

Someone else might have made a joke about going number two, just to break the silence. Not Webb.

He was fine with silence.

Good thing.

When the cop shut the door on Webb, that's all he had for company.

Silence.

FIVE

THEN

A little over a week earlier, Webb had not sat with his mother at his grandfather's funeral. Instead, he'd waited until the service began before he slipped into the back row, noting where she sat with his stepfather, and he had been ready to escape as soon as the service ended.

At the reading of the will in the lawyer's office, three days before his arrival in Norman Wells, Webb didn't have much choice except to sit in clear view of her. She'd given him an imploring look, like she wanted a hug or at least a word from him.

He'd crossed his arms and given a firm shake of his head. It had been months since he had been in the same room as his mother. The death of his grandfather was about the only reason in the world he'd consent to it, but that didn't mean he had to talk to her.

The look on her face when he'd shaken his head broke his heart. It was almost enough to make him run across this room with its dark overstuffed leather chairs and couches, run past all his relatives and their solemn looks. Almost enough to put him on his knees in front of her, clutching her legs and bawling about how much he missed her and how much he wished he could live at home with her like any normal teenager.

That wasn't possible.

Instead, he'd let a couple of tears run down his face without wiping them away. If anyone noticed, they'd think he was grieving for his dead grandfather. Nobody in the room suspected that Webb had left home when he'd been busted with drugs in his locker at school. No, to the rest of the clan, Webb's family was as close-knit as the others, although sometimes he wondered if his grandfather had suspected something was wrong. But there was nothing anyone could have done without making it worse. So the secret remained.

There were twelve people in the lawyer's office— Webb and his mother, his mother's three sisters, two of their husbands, and his five cousins. There was DJ and his twin brother Steve, and Adam and Spencer and Bernard, who insisted on being called Bunny. Webb was pretty sure the only person they all wished could be there was their grandfather.

Webb had learned to be very watchful, and he saw his cousin DJ shudder. He saw DJ's mother reach out and place her hand on DJ's hand.

"It's all right, DJ," she whispered. That's how quiet the office was; even a whisper carried.

Webb sensed his mother was watching him just as closely as Webb was watching his cousins, so he leaned forward, knowing his long hair would cover his face. Webb's hair hung below his shoulders. His stepfather hated that, which was a good enough reason to keep growing it.

After DJ's mother whispered to DJ, all of them sat in silence, waiting for the lawyer to arrive. It had been a term of David McLean's will that all of the grand-sons assemble. Webb had left a voice mail for his mother on her cell phone, saying that he would only go to the lawyer's office if his stepfather wasn't there.

Webb thought this was ironic, the silence. His grandfather would never have allowed it. Silence wasn't an option around David McLean. Laughter, yes. Shouting, yes. Arguing and jokes, yes. Silence, no.

A man in a suit pushed through the doorway, shutting the door behind him and going to the big mahogany desk in the center of the room.

"Good afternoon" he said. "Thank you for coming. My name is John Devine, and I've been David's lawyer for twenty years. This is a very sad day, and I must admit that this was a day I didn't expect to be part of. I'm much younger than David, but even so I expected him to outlive me. He was a man of so much passion. It was a true joy to have known him."

Webb sensed that Devine meant it. And it was totally correct. Grandpa David had been an amazing man, a joy to everyone who met him.

"The terms of the will are both straightforward and, shall we say, most interesting," Mr. Devine said. "And with a most interesting twist. Let's begin with the more conventional parts. All of David's assets—

his home, investments and cottage—are to be divided equally among his daughters. All of these assets, with the exception of the cottage, are to be liquidated and dispersed to the four heirs. The cottage's ownership will be transferred to list his daughters as co-owners. It says, and I quote, 'This was a place of so many great memories shared with my family that I wish it to be used in perpetuity by my grandchildren and their children and their children.'"

Devine paused. "Is that all clear?"

Webb felt more tears on his face. He had great memories of the cottage—weekends and summers spent with his cousins and their parents and Grandpa. All of those memories, though, existed in a different life, the life before Webb's father died of cancer, before his mother married Elliott Skinner.

"Excellent," Mr. Devine said at the murmurs of agreement. "Now I need to set out the next part— the interesting part—of the will. A sum of money— a rather substantial sum—has been put aside to fund an undertaking...or I should say, *seven* undertakings." He paused. "This is without a doubt one of the most unusual clauses that I have ever been asked to put in a will."

He looked slowly from person to person. "I know you are all are anxious to hear about these undertakings. However, I cannot share them with all of you at this moment."

It seemed like everybody began shouting at once. Except for Webb. He just watched.

"Please, please!" Mr. Devine said, cutting through the noise. "You will all be fully informed, but not all of you will be informed at the same time. Some people will have to leave the room prior to the undertakings being read. Therefore, as per the terms of the will, I request that the grandsons—"

"I'm not going anywhere," Steve said. "I don't want to be kicked out of the room."

"You'll go if you're told to go," his twin brother DJ said.

Some things, Webb thought, never change.

"You don't understand," the lawyer said. "He can stay."

"If he's staying, then I'm staying as well," DJ said.

"And me too," Webb said, speaking for the first time. He didn't like attention, but there had been a time when he felt like he and his five cousins were a tribe. He would stand with them here too, if only for all the memories of how great life had been before his stepfather.

The room erupted in noise again.

"Could everybody please just stop!" Devine stood. "Please, I am reading a will. Decorum is needed. Out of respect for the deceased, you all need to follow his directions. Is that understood?"

"Sorry," DJ said.

"Me too," Steve said.

Devine began again. "Before I go on, I need to ask everybody to agree to respect the terms of his will— *all* the terms of his will."

"Of course we agree," DJ's mother said.

Everyone else nodded in agreement.

"Excellent," the lawyer said. "Now I need to have everybody except for the six grandsons leave the room."

"What?" one of the adults said.

"Did you say that the adults have to leave?" someone else asked.

"Yes. Everyone except the grandsons," said Mr. Devine.

SIX

NOW

The jail cell smelled of vomit.

While Webb didn't want to get used to the smell, he was getting used to the changes in scenery. Three days earlier, he'd been in a lawyer's office in a high-rise in Toronto, trying not to look at his mother. The day after that, he'd been in Phoenix, Arizona, facing a dry heat that sucked all traces of sweat off his skin. Yesterday, in Yellowknife, he'd been grounded because of fog.

Naturally, it made him think of his grandpa and why Webb was here in Norman Wells. His grandpa had lived an entire lifetime of adventures.

He'd loved to tell Webb about his exploits. When they'd gotten together to arrange the guitar loan, Webb had been with his grandpa for an entire glorious afternoon, lost in those stories, no different than when he'd been a little boy, loving the sound of his grandpa's voice.

Then, without warning, his grandpa had held Webb's shoulders, looked him in the eye and said, "Life is difficult more often that it is not. To live means to face difficulties. It's what you learn from those difficulties that matters. And Webby, I want you to remember what a German philosopher named Friedrich Nietzsche once said: 'That which does not kill us makes us stronger.'"

It had been a quiet, serious moment. Then, like he did so often, his grandpa had given Webb a big grin, to relieve the seriousness of the moment.

Still, Webb had wondered then and wondered since. Had his grandpa known what had turned him from an eleven-year-old boy who snuggled with his beagle every night into a seventeen-year-old who could turn away from his mother at a funeral?

That which does not kill us makes us stronger.

Had his grandpa known about all the years Webb had been forced to choose between getting stronger or just giving up?

For Webb, it began at age eleven, with simple grains of rice. White rice. Dry. Scattered on the floor at the foot of Webb's bed.

He'd completed his homework at the kitchen table—figuring out square roots of fractions or some other stupid thing that would be no use to him later in life—and gone upstairs to get ready for bed, knowing that his beagle, Niblet, would be there to comfort him through the nightmares that had been constant since his dad had died. At home, Niblet was always beside him. Not one single day had Niblet not been waiting at the gate when Webb came home from school.

Webb had stopped, Niblet by his side, puzzled at the sight of the grains of rice on the gleaming hardwood.

As Webb tried to make sense of why rice would be on his floor, a strong hand pushed him into his room and he heard a *click* as the door was locked.

His stepfather—his new stepfather—had followed Webb inside and shut the door. It had been one year, three weeks and two days since Webb's dad had died from cancer. It had been only two days since the wedding ceremony that had put a new father in Webb's home.

"Sir?" Webb said.

Looking back, Webb knew that he should have realized something was wrong within an hour after the wedding ceremony, when Elliott Skinner, who had started a successful security business after his discharge from the army, had pulled Webb aside and warned him not to call him anything but "sir." Not Father. Not Dad. Not Mr. Skinner. But sir.

"You think you won, don't you?" Elliott said. He reached down and pulled Niblet into his arms.

Elliot Skinner was a medium-sized man, but his posture was perfect and his shoulders always square. It made him seem bigger. He was a handsome man, too, with teeth as perfect as his posture, and expensive suits that matched his smile. Perfection. It was an image everyone trusted.

There was a reason to trust it. Elliott Skinner had been on four tours of duty overseas.

"Sir?"

"Tonight at dinner. When you convinced Charlotte to let you quit soccer and keep taking guitar lessons, you made her choose you over me."

The last gift Webb's dad had given him was the Gibson guitar, a month before the cancer took him. Webb loved the guitar almost as much as he loved his beagle. He loved music too, and he loved the guitar because it had belonged to his dad.

Guitars and rock music, Elliott had explained to Charlotte, did not build character, but instead led to drug use and worse. Soccer taught discipline and teamwork and built a growing boy's body.

"Sir, I—" It bothered Webb that Elliott referred to his mother as Charlotte, not as "your mother." It was as if Elliott wanted to break their bond.

"You will speak when I allow you to speak." Elliott rubbed the top of Niblet's head as he spoke. It was a scary contrast—Elliott's open affection for the dog and his ice-cold voice. "Let me explain to you the difference between a battle and a war. A war consists of many smaller battles between two or more opposing forces. You can win a battle, but in the end, lose a war. By defying me in front of Charlotte, you declared war on me. She chose your side, which means you won the opening battle."

"Sir, I—"

"I want you to change into your soccer uniform," Elliott said. "You will kneel on the rice on bare knees for five minutes. Then you will have an understanding of what happens when you engage in war with me."

While putting on his soccer uniform, Webb had not worried much about what it would mean to kneel on rice. But within ten seconds of placing his full body weight on the rice, the agony had brought tears to his eyes. And he stood up, rubbing his bare knees with his hands to ease the sting.

"You can't make me do this," he told Elliott.

Elliott was still standing inside the locked bedroom, still holding Niblet.

"You can't make me do this, *sir*," Elliott corrected.

"I'm not listening to you," Webb said, anger breaking through his usually peaceful exterior. "You're not my father."

Elliott gave him a silky smile. "I wondered how long it would take you to get there. No, I'm not your father. And yes, I can make you do that."

Elliott continued to stroke the top of Niblet's head. "I believe your father gave you this dog on the first day you went to school. Kindergarten, right? I've seen the photos in your family album."

"Put him down," Webb said, stepping toward Elliott. "You wouldn't hurt him, would you?"

"I didn't say that, did I?" Elliott responded. "Think carefully. This is a significant moment. You need to ask yourself how far I will go to win this war. And remember, I'm a soldier."

Elliott set Niblet on the floor, and the dog raced to Webb, who scooped him up in his arms. Niblet licked his face.

"You'll listen to me?" Elliott asked.

Webb was only eleven, holding the dog he loved. His confusion was a horrible blackness that felt like sinking in mud. Elliott hadn't threatened Niblet directly. No one was crazy enough to hurt a dog, right? Even though he knew that Elliott's threat to hurt Niblet might only be in his imagination, Webb couldn't escape his fears. Webb felt like he hadn't done enough for his dad when he got sick. He still believed that somehow, someway, he could have made a difference, and somehow, someway, he could have helped his dad live longer. So if he hadn't done enough to save his dad, he'd do whatever it took to save Niblet, even against something that might only be an imaginary threat.

Elliott must have seen the confusion in Webb's face, because he gave a perfect smile with those perfect teeth.

"Five minutes on the rice," Elliott said. "You will not say a word of this to Charlotte. And at breakfast tomorrow, you will tell Charlotte you changed your mind and you'd prefer soccer after all. After school, you're going to get a haircut. You look like a girl. Agreed?"

Webb was only eleven but old enough to understand how much his life had just changed.

Elliott must have seen that on Webb's face too, because he gave another perfect smile with those perfect teeth.

"I'm glad you understand me," Elliott said. "Now kneel."

SEVEN

Webb ran his tongue over the hole in his bottom lip where his tooth had been. It hurt. So did the gap in his gums. Even so, it was better than losing an upper tooth. That would be pretty obvious. This way, at least, people wouldn't see a gap, since his lower teeth were always hidden when he smiled.

It was difficult to guess the time without a watch or a cell phone or a window, especially since he was hearing a new guitar riff in his head. He'd been sitting on the bench, imagining his guitar was in his hands and feeling where he'd put his fingers to play the chords.

He even had the hook of a song to go with the riff. He'd been thinking about the playground just outside the walls of his prison cell. The brightly colored bars of the swing set and the teeter-totter were probably less than twenty steps away. So close, so far.

And that's where he was headed with the song's hook.

Take me close
Take me far
But the cages we choose for ourselves
Keep us from what really matters
And you matter most to me
So why are you so close and yet so far…

He was feeling it—the rise of a G chord—when the door opened. It was the cop, his face expressionless.

He pointed out the cell door, and the meaning was clear to Webb. Time to get out.

"I get to make a phone call?" Webb said.

"My advice? Call George to pick you up."

"Right," Webb said. "The guy who had my back at the airport."

"He did," the cop said. "Call him and let him explain."

Webb walked out of the cell and saw Brent in the open area beyond the desk.

Brent was a head taller than the cop, and the extra height allowed Webb a clear view of his face. Or, more accurately, of the white gauze and the purple bruises.

Broken nose, for sure. But Webb didn't need a view of Brent's wrecked face to tell him that. He'd felt Brent's nose crack against his skull.

"I don't want to press charges," Brent said to Webb. "I'm sorry for everything I did to you at the airport. This misunderstanding is entirely my fault."

Brent spoke as if he'd memorized his little speech.

"See?" Webb said to the cop. "Someone should have believed me a lot earlier."

"Yeah," the cop said in a flat voice. He turned to Brent. "You're full of crap, and we both know it."

"I fell and hit my nose on the baggage carousel," Brent said. "All a misunderstanding."

"Nothing like a good believable story to keep everyone happy," the cop said.

"Yup," Brent said. "Need me to sign a paper or am I good to go?"

"Stay away from this kid," the cop said. "Understand?"

"Don't know what you're talking about," Brent said. "All a misunderstanding."

The station phone rang. When no one answered, the cell phone on the cop's belt rang. Like the call to the station had been forwarded.

The cop waved his hand, and Brent walked out of the station as the cop answered his phone.

The cop listened, then said, "Thanks for calling me back, George. You should get here right away. I can't hold the kid any longer."

When he hung up, he walked to the other side of the office, where Webb's guitar case was leaning against the wall.

He picked it up and handed it to Webb.

"We're almost done here," the cop said. "I'll get the rest of your stuff."

"I'm not waiting for George," Webb said. "Fact is, I'm going to look for another guide."

"Nobody better than George. He tells me you want to hike the Canol. He's the guy for you."

"The guy who pretended he didn't see a thing at the airport? What's he going to do if a grizzly shows up?"

The cop shook his head. "Brent—the guy whose nose you busted—has already spent four years in prison for aggravated assault. That's not the worst of it. At a work camp last summer, two guys disappeared. Got lost, nobody could find them. That's the official story. Unofficially? Brent had a grudge against both of them."

"You're telling me Brent killed two people?"

"Nope. That would be slander. I am telling you if there was the slightest bit of proof that he was involved in how they disappeared, he'd be behind bars. He's psycho in the worst way possible—a way impossible to prove. George knows that just as much as anybody else in this town. We all breathe easier when Brent is gone."

"How about what happened at the airport? That's not enough reason to put him in here?"

The cop let out a long breath. "Let's say, in theory, that Brent took the first swing at you. And let's say, in theory, that I put him in a cell instead of you. I'd have to let him make a phone call, because if I didn't, his lawyer would be all over me. And his lawyer's a real pain."

"How do you know mine isn't?"

"Let me finish. I throw Brent in here and he'd be out in five hours. And there would only be one thing on his mind. Finding you. In a small town like this, that would take him less than an hour. Which means that six hours after throwing Brent in a cell, you'd be at the clinic. Or worse, flown out to the emergency unit at the hospital in Yellowknife. Or even worse, you wouldn't even be found. There's a lot of wilderness out there, and Brent knows it well enough to find a place to hide your body." He paused for a second and looked Webb in the eye. "Much easier to keep you safe by not letting you out. You're a kid. Your parents aren't going to be upset once they hear that I was trying to protect you, which is why I was prepared to keep you from calling a lawyer. Brent's not stupid. He came in and did what he did so I'd have to let you out. Told me if I didn't, his lawyer would be calling. I didn't have much choice. Could you do me a favor and stay here the night anyway? I'll make sure you get a great meal."

"No," Webb said. He was done with letting people scare him.

"Then the next best thing is for you to let George take you for the night. He wanted you in here to make sure there was no hassle, because he doesn't need to spend the next five years wondering if Brent will stab him in the back some night. Too late for that now, so George is willing to take that risk to keep you safe."

"Nice," Webb said. "So if something happens to George someday, it's because of me. No thanks. Call George and tell him I'll see him tomorrow at the helicopter. I'll fight my own battles."

"Not smart, kid."

"I've dealt with worse," Webb said.

That which does not kill us makes us stronger.

The cop shrugged.

Webb pulled his guitar out of the case while the cop got some paperwork ready.

Webb could still hear the riff in his head and he wanted to try it on real strings. But the cop still had Webb's guitar picks.

Webb thought of something and rooted around in the back pocket of his jeans.

He hit the first few chords hard, and they sounded great.

The cop lifted his head and gave Webb a half smile. He didn't have to say it. Webb could tell he liked it.

Then the cop frowned. "That's not a guitar pick."

"Nope," Webb said. "You've got all of them."

Webb hit the chords again. Riffed a little more.

Not bad, Webb thought, even though I had to use my tooth for a guitar pick.

EIGHT

The entire downtown of Norman Wells was within a block of the police station. Not much here, Webb thought. A couple of restaurants. Couple of hotels. He checked into one of them and left his guitar in the room when he went out to explore the town.

Webb knew that in a town of seven hundred, there was no point in expecting steel and glass skyscrapers and traffic lights and crowds thick enough to hide pickpockets. There was no shame in being small.

In comparison to what was around it though, Norman Wells was just as impressive as Toronto. Given the thousands and thousands and thousands of square kilometers of uninhabited wilderness, a collection of seven hundred people was a welcome metropolis.

Webb had watched the bush and trees and water pass beneath the Canadian North jet all the way from Yellowknife, and what struck him most was the complete lack of roads outside of Norman Wells.

When he pictured wilderness, there were usually roads in and out and around the bush and trees and water.

Not here.

You want out?

You fly.

Or travel up or down the Mackenzie River on a barge.

Or walk.

Winter, you want out?

You fly.

Or travel down winter roads cut through the bush or on the Mackenzie River on the ice highway north of Yellowknife.

Or walk.

Webb knew all of this from the websites he'd googled on his iPod, but it had a lot more impact up close. All that bush and water, filled with bears and moose and wolves.

Which made what was ahead of him seem even scarier.

One hundred and ten kilometers of walking.

The store—appropriately called The Northern—smelled weird.

Webb stepped inside and saw shelves packed with groceries and a bewildering variety of items, from DVDs to canned peaches to red long johns.

One section had all the stuff he needed to walk a hundred and ten kilometers through a bear-filled, wolf-infested, roadless wilderness.

Webb took a nylon backpack from the wall. Not the kind kids use for hauling stuff to and from school, but one with an aluminum frame that could carry a hundred pounds if needed.

A hundred pounds of rocks.

He took it to the front counter and pulled one of the bank cards out of his wallet.

The guy behind the counter had a leathery, wrinkled face; it looked as if he'd walked to the Yukon and back dozens of times.

Webb put the card on the counter. He had the bank cards to cover any and all expenses that he might face on the journey. Mr. Devine had said that he was allowed to keep whatever was left over after his trip, so the less he spent now, the better. Maybe he'd be able to pay off his guitar. Buy some decent clothes.

"Happy to hold the pack here while you get the rest of what you need," the old man said, his voice sounding like the rumble of a train coming from the far side of a long tunnel. "You don't need to leave your card on the counter to reserve it or anything."

Webb knew the guy could tell he wasn't a regular here. Of course, in a town of seven hundred, you'd know who lived here and who didn't.

"How much time you spend in the bush?" Webb asked.

"You mean over the last forty years?"

It was all Webb needed for an answer.

"All I want right now is the backpack," Webb said. "I'll come back for the rest later."

The man grunted and swiped the bank card. His machine spat out a slip of paper. Webb took it from him before the man could check the balance on the card. Webb didn't want anyone else knowing how much money he was carrying around, even if it wasn't cash.

"'You have any idea what the rest is going to be?" the man behind the counter asked.

"Just what I've read about online," Webb said. "My guess is you know much better than any website what it would take to last a week or two out there. Could you help me?"

The man looked hard at Webb, before extending his hand across the counter.

"Name's Joey Nicol. Glad to help."

Webb shook his hand but didn't offer his own name. "I need supplies for two weeks of hiking," he said. "Nothing more. I hate carrying more than I have to."

When he'd lived on the street, the older men and women stole shopping carts to keep their stuff in.

Not Webb. If you couldn't run carrying it, no sense owning it.

"Smart," Joey said. "Not many people figure that out until they are on the trail. My advice? Don't get it unless you are going to use it every day. I had a couple of German tourists in here buying a bunch of stuff they might only use once or twice on the whole trip. Like a solar camp shower. Sounds good when you're in the store, but not after you've carried it for ten miles. I couldn't even talk them out of a heavy-duty flashlight, even though we've got twenty-four hours of daylight this time of year."

Webb nodded, picked up the backpack and headed toward the door.

"Hey," Joey said. "Watch out for Brent Melrose. I heard you broke his nose."

Webb stopped, half turned and shrugged like he didn't know what Joey meant.

"Bulldozer mechanic. We all know what he's like. Spent five years in jail after busting up a guy in a bar fight."

So this was life in a small town. Everyone knowing your business.

"Sure," Webb said. "I'll watch out for him."

"You don't sound worried. You should be. Someone said his girlfriend got back on the south-bound jet and left town."

Webb smiled. It felt good to hear that.

"Nothing funny about it," Joey said, obviously not understanding Webb's smile. "You cost him his girlfriend and you busted his nose. He'll run you down like a dog if he can."

"Okay, I'm worried now," Webb said. But not too worried. He'd been beaten up before and had learned he could handle it.

Webb put his hand on the door, but Joey wasn't finished.

"Not one person in town's sorry to hear about what happened at the airport," he said. "So thanks."

NINE

The truck that began following Webb down Raven Street half an hour later did not belong to a bulldozer mechanic who had spent five years in jail for busting a guy up in a bar fight.

It belonged to the cop. Twenty meters behind Webb. Keeping his cop truck at a pace that matched Webb's.

Webb turned right on Mackenzie Drive.

So did the cop, twenty meters behind.

Webb passed the museum. This was his third time past it. It was on his to-do list, and after he was finished walking around with stones in his backpack, he would spend as much time there as he could before it closed. He'd seen online that it would have lots of information for what was ahead.

The cop stayed behind Webb. Driving at a walking pace. Pretty boring, but being a small-town cop must be like that.

The cop was messing with the next verse of Webb's jail song. He couldn't concentrate.

Webb stopped walking.

The cop stopped driving.

Webb walked back toward him.

The cop stayed put.

Webb reached the truck.

The cop had the window open on his side.

"How do you pronounce your name?" Webb asked, looking at the cop's nametag. "It seems like we're getting to know each other, and I want to stop thinking of you as 'the cop.'"

"Sil-veh."

"Not Sil-vann?" Webb asked. "Or Sil-vain. It's spelled S-Y-L-V-A-I-N."

"The *n* is silent."

"Sil-vah," Webb said.

"Not vaah. Veh. Like ven, except like you are hinting that the *n* is there. Didn't you ever take French in school?"

Webb tried it again.

"Much better." Sylvain grinned.

"Well," Webb said, "I have a taxpayer's complaint. It's about the gas and time that the police force in this town is wasting. Where should I file that complaint?"

"Police station," Sylvain said. "I think you know where it is."

"Excellent," Webb said. "How about you drive up there, and I'll meet you as soon as I can?"

"No. How about I just keep following you till you get there?"

"How about not?"

"Because as soon as I'm gone, you'll head the other way and disappear," Sylvain said. "I need to stay close because when Brent Melrose finds you, it will get ugly. And he will find you. Only took ten minutes for someone to call the police station about a suspicious guy walking up and down carrying a big backpack."

"Maybe I'll file a harassment charge against you then."

"I don't think so. That would mean another trip to the station, and you don't like dealing with cops. Which is why you would disappear as soon as I drove away. If I did. Which I won't."

"You don't know me that well," Webb said. "We just met. I couldn't even pronounce your name right."

"You can now. And I know you aren't a taxpayer. Buskers don't pay taxes."

Webb glared at him.

Sylvain just smiled. "Living on the streets," he said. "No home. Just a guitar and the money you make when people throw cash in your guitar case." Another smile. "Your stepfather likes to talk. He said he had you followed for a while, just so he knew what you were doing. He runs a security firm, right?"

"Please," Webb said, "call him Elliott. Hard not to puke when I'm reminded that he married my mother." It wasn't the cop's business that he didn't live on the street anymore.

"Elliott likes to talk. Says you have a first name too. Jim. Where's your guitar, Jim?"

"Hotel."

"Stay with George tonight. It will be better for you."

"Not for George."

"Then I guess I'll keep following you," Sylvain continued. "Just so you know."

"That changes things," Webb said. "A lot. Can I jump in the back of your truck and catch a ride back to the Northern?"

Sylvain nodded and Webb jumped in.

When Sylvain slowed for the next corner—like Webb knew he would because Webb had walked this stretch three times already, Sylvain right behind him—Webb threw his backpack out, then jumped out after it. It took a lot of effort to hoist the backpack and run, but he made it into the trees and disappeared from sight before Sylvain could stop the truck and get back to the spot where Webb had bailed.

If Brent was looking for a fight, Webb thought, it would be better to deal with it now when he could see it coming.

TEN

THEN

In Toronto, in the lawyer's high-rise office, three days before Webb's arrival in Norman Wells, Mr. Devine addressed all six grandsons in the vacuum after all the adults had left the room.

"Well, gentlemen," he said, "I'm assuming that nobody saw this coming."

"Grandpa was always full of surprises," Bunny said.

"So I guess because of that we're *not* that surprised," Steve added.

"Interesting perspective," the lawyer said. "The only way you would have been surprised is if he didn't do something to surprise you."

"Pretty much," Steve said.

"So if he'd done nothing, then you would have actually been surprised, which wouldn't have been a surprise. Sort of a Catch-22, don't you think?"

"Do you think, sir, that we could go on?" DJ said. "I believe we're all anxious to hear what you're going to tell us."

Webb was happy to simply watch. Whatever was going to happen was going to happen, regardless of what he did or said.

"I'm sure you are," Devine answered DJ. "But actually, *I'm* not going to tell you anything." He paused. "Your *grandfather* is. I'm going to play a video your grandfather made."

The lawyer walked over to a television in a big cabinet. He turned to face the six grandsons. "I was in the room when your grandfather recorded this. I think *all* of you will be at least a little surprised by what he has to say."

He turned the TV on and there was Webb's grandpa.

"I'm not sure why I have to be wearing makeup," David McLean said, turning to face somebody off camera. "This is my will, not some late-night talk show…and it's certainly not a *live* taping."

Someone in the room with his grandpa laughed.

"Good morning…or afternoon, boys," he began. "If you are watching this, I must be dead, although on this fine afternoon I feel very much alive. I want to start off by saying that I don't want you to be too sad. I had a good life and I wouldn't change a minute of it. That said, I still hope that you are at least a little sad and that you miss having me around. After all, I was one *spectacular* grandpa!"

His cousins started laughing, and Webb joined in. It felt good. He didn't laugh much anymore.

"And you were simply the best grandsons a man could ever have. I want you to know that of all the joys in my life, you were among my greatest. From the first time I met each of you to the last moments I spent with you—and of course I don't know what those last moments were, but I know they were wonderful—I want to thank you all for being part of my life. A very big, special, wonderful, warm part of my life."

The old man took a sip of water. Webb noticed his hand shaking. He must have been nervous.

"I wanted to record this rather than just have my lawyer read it out to you. Hello, Johnnie."

"Hello, Davie," Devine replied.

"Johnnie, I hope you appreciate that twenty-year-old bottle of Scotch I left you," his grandpa said. "And you better not have had more than one snort of it before the reading of my will! But knowing you the way I do, I suspect you would have had two."

"He did know me well," Devine said.

"I just wanted—needed—to say goodbye to all of you boys in person, or at least as in person as this allows." On the television screen, David took another sip from his glass. His hand was still shaking.

Webb found that significant. He'd never seen his grandpa nervous. David McLean had lived into his nineties, strong and healthy. His hands had never shaken before.

"Life is an interesting journey," David said from the television, "one that seldom takes you where you think you might be going. Certainly I never expected that I was going to become an old man. In fact, there were more than a few times when I was a boy that I didn't believe I was going to live to see another day, never mind live long enough to grow old."

This was a man who'd been a pilot in World War II, been shot at over France, had had adventures all over the world. Webb knew that the man on the television screen was not exaggerating.

"But I did live a long and wonderful life. I was blessed to meet the love of my life, your grandmother Vera. It is so sad that she passed on before any of you had a chance to meet her. I know people never speak ill of the dead—and I'm counting on you all to keep up that tradition with me—but your grandmother was simply the most *perfect* woman in the world."

Webb's own mother—David's daughter, Charlotte— was close to perfect too. At least she had been when Webb's dad was alive. He bit back a heavy sigh, thinking of his mother outside the lawyer's office. So close. But truly, so far away.

"Her only flaw," David continued, "as far as I can see, was being foolish enough to marry me. She gave me not only a happy life, but four daughters...four amazing daughters. I just wish she could have been there to watch them grow into the four wonderful women who became your mothers."

Webb's grandmother had died when the girls were young—the youngest, Aunt Vicky, was only four at the time. David McLean had raised the girls on his own. Webb wished his mother had followed that same path when his dad had died when Webb was ten.

"I was always comforted by the thought that I believed she was watching them too," David said from the television. "Sitting up there in heaven or wherever. I guess as you're hearing this, I have an answer to that question. I pray that I'm with her now."

He raised his glass again and toasted his grandsons. "Being both father and mother to my girls meant that I was always running fast to try and do everything. Sometimes the need to earn a living got in the way of me being there for my daughters. There were too many school plays, violin recitals and soccer games that I never got to. And that was why I made a point to be there for almost every one of your games and school events and concerts. This was both a promise I made and a complete joy. You boys, you wonderful, incredible, lovely boys have been such a blessing…seven blessings. Some blessings come later than others."

Seven? Webb squinted, as if looking harder at the screen would help his hearing. Six. There were six grandsons. Obviously a mistake, but he didn't give it much thought because he wanted to give his grandpa his full attention.

"But I didn't bring you here simply to tell you how much I loved you all. Being part of your lives was one of the greatest achievements of my life, and I wouldn't trade it for anything, but being there for all your big moments meant that I couldn't be elsewhere. I've done a lot, but it doesn't seem that time is going to permit me the luxury of doing everything I wished for. So, I have some requests, some *last* requests. In the possession of my lawyer are some envelopes. One for each of you."

Webb glanced at Mr. Devine, who stood at the side of the room holding envelopes fanned out like playing cards.

"Each of these requests, these tasks," David continued, "has been specifically selected for you to fulfill. All of the things you will need to complete your task will be provided—money, tickets, guides. Everything. I am not asking any of you to do anything stupid or unnecessarily reckless—certainly nothing as stupid or reckless as I did at your ages. Your parents may be worried, but I have no doubts. Just as I have no doubts that you will all become fine young men.

I am sad that I will not be there to watch you all grow into the incredible men I know you will become. But I don't need to be there to know that will happen. I am so certain of that. As certain as I am that I will be there with you as you complete my last requests, as you continue your life journeys."

On the television screen, he lifted up his glass again.

"A final toast. To the best grandsons a man could ever have. I love you all so much. Good luck."

The video ended and his grandpa was gone.

ELEVEN

NOW

It didn't make Webb feel any better that Sylvain had been correct in saying it wouldn't take long for Brent Melrose to find him.

When a kid on a mountain bike approached Webb on the path through the trees, Webb was thinking about bears. And how all his previous ideas about cleverly climbing a nearby tree to escape a bear were not so clever after all.

First of all, Webb knew that grizzlies can't climb trees, but black bears can.

That was good. If you have a choice between out-climbing a grizzly or out-climbing a black bear, it's the grizzly you want to out-climb. Grizzlies are huge—not that black bears are tiny—and more unpredictable and bad tempered.

Webb also knew that if you're attacked by a female grizzly it's better to play dead. But with male grizzlies, you are supposed to fight like crazy and hope for the best. Hit them on the nose, scream and kick. Prove to the male that messing with you is a mistake.

As if a 150-pound human is going to make a 600-pound grizzly think that it's a mistake to get into a fight. Sure. And Elvis is still eating donuts, and the Toronto Maple Leafs are going to win a Stanley Cup one day.

But second—and to Webb, this was the crucial issue—how do you know whether you are being attacked by a male or female grizzly? Yes, if the grizzly is with a couple of cubs, go ahead and assume it's female. Other than that, how are you going to know? Wait until you are on the ground trapped underneath it and then reach down and see if there's anything to grab?

Like that would put a male grizzly in a better mood.

All Webb's research about bears in the north, at least when it came to trees, had been wasted though.

Norman Wells wasn't very far south of the tree line, the point in the Arctic where trees won't grow. The spruce trees on the path were barely higher than his head, and the trunks of the trees were skinnier than his arms. Climbing to the top would only put him at the perfect level for a bear to chomp on his butt.

Turns out, too, that Webb should have been more worried about the kid on the mountain bike.

The kid, who looked about twelve, stopped in front of Webb. Short dark hair. Freckles. Jeans. Blue hoodie. And attitude.

"Hey," Webb said. He shifted his pack on his back. It still felt a little heavy. He had gone down to the Mackenzie River and put rocks into his backpack earlier. He had started with the backpack half full and had been taking them out, one at a time, dropping them along the road as he walked the streets of Norman Wells.

"You the guy who just landed here with a guitar?" the kid said.

"Strictly speaking, the plane landed. I was on it."

"With a guitar?"

"With a guitar," Webb said.

"Good. You just made me a hundred bucks."

The kid turned his bike around and pedaled about twenty steps back up the trail. Then he stopped the bike and faced Webb again. He pulled a walkie-talkie off his belt, held it to his mouth and stared at Webb while he clicked the side button.

Webb heard the chime, and then the kid said, "Found him. On the path. Headed toward Raven Road." He released the button.

The walkie-talkie crackled. "Keep him in sight. I'm driving that way." A man's voice.

"You're kidding me," Webb said. "You're a bounty hunter?"

"Hundred bucks," the kid said. "Not gonna turn that down."

His walkie-talkie crackled again. A kid's voice this time. "Joey, remember our deal. Whoever finds him splits with the others."

Then another kid's voice. "Yeah, man. That's like thirty bucks each."

"Three of you," Webb said.

"Brent Melrose, he's someone you don't mess with. It was either take the money or always be on the run in this town. Nothing personal, you know."

"Makes me feel a lot better," Webb said.

At the airport, he'd been able to surprise Melrose, who was so much bigger than him that surprise was about the only weapon Webb had.

And now that element of surprise was gone.

Still, better to see the fight coming than to get stabbed in the back.

Webb wondered if it would be better to take the fight to the woods instead of the road. He stepped off the path into boggy ground. Branches tore at his backpack. The trees were short and skinny but close together. No way to run from a bear in this stuff, and, as a predator, Melrose was worse than a bear. The thickness of the bush also made it a bad place to fight.

Webb heard the walkie-talkie chime again, then the first kid's voice. "He's in the trees."

"Follow him," came the reply. "Let me know where he is at all times. He's going to have to come out somewhere."

This was true, but Webb had a rough idea of the layout of the town in his head. When he'd jumped off the truck, he'd known he wasn't in the wilderness. This area was framed by the streets of Norman Wells.

Moving through the bush was loud and progress was slow. The kid on the bike would have no trouble following, and Webb wouldn't be able to escape.

Webb took a deep breath and turned back to the path.

When he got there, the kid gave him a respectful distance.

"Don't worry," Webb told the kid, "I'm not going to do anything to you."

Webb could have reversed direction and gone back to where he'd jumped out of the truck, maybe get some help from passing traffic, but it would only have been relative safety. Because, until Webb got out of Norman Wells, it seemed like Melrose was going to find him.

So Webb continued walking in the opposite direction. He was going to face Brent alone and get this over with.

That was the one good thing about having a stepfather who tortured you. Soon enough, pain didn't bother you that much.

TWELVE

The path twisted and turned through the short spruce trees and came out on a quiet road, where Brent Melrose was leaning against a black truck with beefed-up tires. He took a swig from a bottle of beer.

The kid on the bike had stayed behind Webb the entire time he trudged up the path, reporting Webb's progress on his walkie-talkie every thirty seconds. Webb hadn't seen any sense in trying to shut him up. What was he going to do, turn and hurt the kid if he didn't?

Not Webb's style.

Besides, Webb could see some humor in the situation as the kid kept repeating the same message.

"This is Corey. Come in?" *Crackle, crackle, pause.* "Yeah, he's still headed your way. Out."

"This is Corey. Come in?" *Crackle, crackle, pause.* "Yeah, he's still headed your way. Out."

"This is Corey. Come in?" *Crackle, crackle, pause.* "Yeah, he's still headed your way. Out."

As Webb came to the end of the path, he took his backpack off and leaned it against a tree. He walked toward Brent's truck. Slowly.

"See what you did to my face?" Brent asked.

"I thought it was all a misunderstanding. You fell into the luggage. Isn't that what you said at the station?"

"The cop was right. That was crap," Brent said. When he breathed, a strange whistling sound came from his nose. It looked—and sounded—painful.

He was swaying some, and Webb hoped he wasn't too drunk to listen to sense. He held up his iPod, switched it to record video and pointed it at Brent.

"Four thirty-five," Webb said clearly. "Standing here on—" Webb turned to the kid on the bike. "What's this road?"

"Don't know. Down at the corner, though, if you turn toward the river, that's where the school principal lives. Does that help?"

"Standing just down from the principal's house," Webb said. "Just for the record, we've got full video happening here."

"Put that away," Brent said. "Or I'll rip it out of your hands."

"Not too interested in that," Webb answered.

Brent took a lumbering step toward Webb. "I said give it to me. It's payback time."

Brent charged.

It didn't take much effort to step aside. Brent's momentum took him past Webb like a bull missing a matador. Difference was, Webb wasn't using a red cape and didn't have a short stabbing sword to finish Brent off when he got tired.

Webb kept the camera on Brent. He had lots of memory left. Could probably video the next half hour if he had too.

Brent swung around, grunted and charged again, swinging his arms in a futile attempt to wrap them around Webb.

Webb could have tripped him but just let him go past again.

Brent almost fell into his truck but caught his balance in time.

"How about we just call this quits," Webb said. "You have better things to do. Same with me."

"And let people talk about how some long-haired-musician type busted my nose and got away with it?"

Brent obviously thought he was clever, charging again as he finished speaking. Like Webb would be so dazzled by his insult, he'd forget to notice. Thing was, Webb had his eyes on the center of Brent's chest. Anybody can fake moves, but no matter how good the fake, the center of the chest was where the body went. Another thing he had learned the hard way.

Brent blew past Webb and took a few more steps to stop. Already getting tired.

He leaned on his knees, near Webb's backpack.

"Look at this," he said. "Somebody left something behind."

Clever, Webb thought, as Brent hefted the backpack and said, "What a shame we need to see what's inside."

Really clever.

Brent lifted the flap and turned the pack upside down, like he was expecting Webb to get mad.

What Brent didn't expect were rocks. A lot of them, each about the size of a fist.

"Rocks?" Brent was dumbfounded. "Rocks?"

Webb almost laughed. Brent had successfully identified the dull round objects polished smooth by centuries in the river.

"Rocks," Brent said one more time. "What kind of idiot carries rocks in his backpack?" He grinned and picked one up in his right hand. "But thanks," he said. "You're making it too easy."

He fired the rock at Webb's head. Webb ducked.

There was a crash as glass shattered. To Webb, it was a very satisfying sound. The rock must have hit the only glass nearby—the side window of Brent's truck, which was directly behind Webb.

Webb didn't turn to admire the damage though. Not when Brent had a pile of rocks within reach.

Besides, it wasn't necessary. The expression on Brent's face—or what Webb could see beyond the bandages—said it all. Horror and rage. Obviously the sound of broken glass had been a lot less satisfying to Brent than to Webb.

"Arrgghhh!" Brent dropped his head and charged at Webb again.

Webb began to feel cold rage engulf him, the cold rage that sustained him whenever his stepfather had hurt him. It was a horrible feeling, being certain that, if given the chance, he would take Brent's truck and drive over Brent without any remorse or regrets. Just the way he knew that, if given the chance, he would hurt Elliott in ways far worse than anything Elliott had ever done to him.

As Brent charged, Webb stepped aside again, but this time left his leg in the way. Brent, blinded by alcohol, anger and bandages, tripped and fell forward, his head thunking into the side of the truck's door.

Webb was surprised that Brent didn't just drop. Instead, he wheeled in a tight circle, as if one of his feet was nailed to the ground, holding his head with both hands.

The head-shaped dent in Brent's door was impressive.

"Come in, come in." Corey spoke into the walkie-talkie. Excited. "Everybody, get here as fast as you can. You have to see this. Brent Melrose is beating the crap out of his own truck."

Webb grabbed a rock and, filled with rage, was ready to move in on Brent and smash him in the head. He stopped when he noticed Sylvain heading toward them in the police truck with his blue-and-reds flashing.

Webb dropped the rock and concentrated on letting his sanity return.

THIRTEEN

About half an hour later, Webb walked back into The Northern with his backpack on.

Joey gave him a big grin. "Heard about you and Brent Melrose. Heard he lost a fight with his truck."

Small town. News traveled fast. But really, it was no different than being in a big city where a small group of people all knew each other. If someone got busted or beat up, everyone knew about it right away.

"It was a nice truck," Webb said. "Now, not so nice."

"He's not going to quit," Joey said.

"I'll be away," Webb said. "I'm not worried."

Webb pointed at all the gear Joey had set aside for him. "Thanks for your help."

"Sure," Joey said. "All together, it costs—"

"Sorry," Webb interrupted him. "First we need to weigh something. You got bathroom scales?"

Joey was obviously puzzled, but he pointed Webb to the household goods aisle.

Webb set a brand-new bathroom scale on the floor and pulled his boots off. "Don't want to get it dirty," he told Joey.

In his socks, with his backpack on, Webb stepped on the scale and noted the weight. He'd refilled his pack with rocks after his encounter with Brent.

Then he took the backpack off and weighed himself again. The difference was fifty-four pounds.

"All I'm going to allow myself is fifty-four pounds," Webb said to Joey. "So if the gear you put together weighs more than that, we need to pull out what's least important."

Joey still looked puzzled, so Webb explained. "I spent an hour walking around with rocks in my pack to find out how much I could carry without hurting myself. I don't want to carry any more than that out there on the trail. I'll be walking for at least a week, and I'm not into unnecessary pain."

Joey grinned. "Okay, now I'm impressed. Most people start with too much and either throw it away on the trail or stagger around out there, wrecking their backs and feet. Let's start filling your backpack and see what will fit."

"Hang on," Webb said. He reached into the backpack and lifted out two of the bigger rocks. He hefted them, comparing the weight in his mind to the weight of his guitar. Seemed about the same. Not quite enough.

"Have a bag?" he asked Joey.

"Sure." Joey didn't ask why, just watched.

Webb put a few more rocks in the bag and lifted it, closing his eyes and imagining his guitar.

Much closer. He set the bag on scale. The rocks weighed sixteen pounds. He thought he might be off by a few pounds either way, but close enough.

"Thirty-eight pounds," Webb said. "That's all I can take. Forgot about my guitar."

"You're taking a guitar on the trail?"

"Yeah." And plenty of guitar strings. Busting a string and not having a replacement would have been disaster. Fortunately, the strings didn't weigh much.

"Sixteen pounds of gear is a lot to give up for a guitar," Joey said.

Webb thought about what the guitar represented to him, and what he'd had to do to have the freedom to play it.

"It might be for some people," he said. "But I'm good with it."

FOURTEEN

In his hotel room, Webb took a small plastic bag and put some wooden matches in it. He slipped the sealed bag of matches into his money belt.

Then he practiced packing and repacking all his gear. The Wi-Fi connection gave him good access to the Internet on his iPod, and he'd just finished reading an article on hiking that advised putting all the heavy stuff as close to the bottom of the backpack as possible. The article also said that keeping some matches dry was a cheap insurance policy.

After the tenth time he refilled his backpack, he realized he was doing it out of nervousness, so he moved to a chair in the corner and picked up his guitar.

He didn't start playing but just held it because it made him feel better.

He began to mentally poke at his nervousness, in the same way he used his tongue to poke at the hole where his tooth used to be.

Was he nervous because he'd be walking a trail in one of the most remote spots in the world? No, he told himself. Knowing that George had lied to try and protect him from Brent gave Webb a sense of comfort. He could trust the older man; the guide would be there to help.

Was he nervous because of Brent?

He gave that serious thought. If the man had actually killed and buried two men out in the wilderness, any rational person would be afraid of Brent. But there was no reason to be afraid tonight.

Sylvain had locked Brent up for the night, at least, expecting that Brent's lawyer would not be able to get him out until sometime the next day. By then,

Webb would have left Norman Wells, safe from the guy Sylvain had called a psycho. Webb had a lot of experience with psychos.

When he was fourteen, his stepfather had come home unexpectedly, catching Webb in front of the television, playing his guitar in sync with the Rolling Stones on a music video.

Elliott turned the television off and faced Webb. The silence—after the loud music from the television—seemed to echo in the room.

"I told Charlotte that I forgot my wallet," Elliott said. "Can't pay for dinner without it. I left her there at the restaurant and told her I'd be right back."

Third anniversary. Dinner at a fancy restaurant. Webb was old enough not to need a babysitter, and he had expected them to be gone for hours.

Standing in front of the couch, guitar in his hands, Webb glanced out the front window at the darkness.

"I parked down the street," Elliott said. "Headlights would have been obvious. Didn't want you slipping away as I came up the driveway."

Because that's exactly what Webb would have done: slip out the back door, into the backyard and through the gate near where Niblet was buried. Instead, Elliott had caught Webb watching MTV. The Rolling Stones. Long-haired musicians who had definitely taken drugs.

"Nothing to say?" Elliott asked.

It had ripped out Webb's heart to bury his beagle. Maybe once a month, Elliott had found an excuse to make Webb kneel on rice grains to protect Niblet. Elliott had not once hurt the dog. Webb had never given Elliott reason to. In the end, a stomach virus had taken Niblet.

"Nothing to say?" Elliott repeated.

Webb reached down. Picked up the remote. Clicked on the television again. Mick Jagger answered Elliott instead. The music was satisfyingly loud. And there was a great closeup of Mick and his thick long hair. A combination sure to irritate Elliott. Much as it hurt not to have Niblet waiting at the gate anymore, Elliott no longer had a hold over Webb.

Can't get no satisfaction.

Keith Richards was Webb's guitar hero. The opening of "Satisfaction" was just a three-note guitar riff. Then some bass. Then drums and acoustic guitar. But the three-note riff drove that song, made it what it was. Webb could play all of it now. But never at home.

Can't get no satisfaction.

Elliott gave his cold smile. He briefly turned his back to Webb to unplug the television, and then in the new silence, through the cold smile that did not waver, he said, "Drop your guitar. Sit on the couch. Take off the sock on your right foot."

"Niblet is gone," Webb said. "You can't do anything to me now or I'll report it."

"Not once did I hurt your dog," Elliott said. "I just want us to be a happy family. All of us. You. Me. And Charlotte. I really want her to remain happy."

Webb felt like he couldn't breathe, and that sudden weakness took away his ability to speak.

Webb sat on the couch and did as commanded.

Webb felt that horrible blackness again, the feeling of sinking into mud he'd felt years earlier when Elliott first made him kneel on rice. Elliott wasn't making a threat about his mom, was he? It was just Webb's imagination, his fear rising like this because he loved his mom so much. Right?

"Hold your right leg straight out in front of you and keep it there."

Webb waited like that as Elliott walked to the kitchen and then returned with a broom. Elliott snapped the broom handle in half and gently slapped the rounded side of the broken piece against the sole of Webb's foot. It was a gentle slap, but Webb still felt it like a sharp and unexpected electrical current.

Elliott spoke in his silky voice, the voice that Webb only heard him use when the two of them were alone. "Amazing, isn't it, how sensitive nerve endings are in the skin of your sole. Won't leave a mark. I expect not to have to do it again. Am I understood? I'm trying to teach you to be a man, and I hope we are past physical punishment."

Webb nodded.

"I want to hear you say it."

"You are understood."

"Not enough."

"You are understood, sir."

"Good," Elliott said. "I've learned that you've been taking guitar lessons even though I expressly forbade it. Tomorrow, I will watch as you smash your guitar in the garage with a hammer. I want you to think about this all night and all through school tomorrow. As you think about it, remember you will never defy me again."

"My dad gave me the guitar." Webb hated that he began crying. "It's all that he left me. Leave the guitar. I'll do anything."

"Tomorrow, I will watch you smash the guitar at my command. And then you sign up for cadets and begin military training. Agreed?"

Webb realized he wasn't afraid of Elliott hurting the soles of his feet. Webb had learned he could deal with pain, and Elliott had just said they were past anything physical. He was terrified, though, of losing what he loved. His dad had been taken unexpectedly and unfairly. Niblet was gone. That left only his mom.

Webb had to protect her at all costs. "Yes, sir," Webb said through his tears. "Agreed."

But in the end, hadn't he hurt his mother far more by leaving home a few years later without a word of explanation?

In the hotel room, guitar across his lap, Webb realized he wasn't feeling nervous. Dealing with Brent earlier in the day had brought back way too many memories about dealing with his stepfather.

He'd abandoned his mother because he believed he needed to protect her.

He knew of only one way to deal with that kind of pain.

Softly, so it wouldn't disturb anyone in the rooms on either side, he strummed the guitar and lost himself in a song he'd written a few months earlier called "Monsters." He sang the first verse under his breath.

Under the bed
What's in my head
That I can't see
You walk the halls
I hear your steps
You haunt my dreams

FIFTEEN

THEN

Two days before his arrival in Norman Wells, Webb had leaned forward in the backseat of a Phoenix taxicab to catch the view through the windshield as a large double-sided gate swung open to reveal palm trees growing in a divider down the center of a wide boulevard. The security code he'd been given worked; so far, at least, the plan was on track, even though he didn't know what the plan was.

It was five in the afternoon. Webb should have been tired. He'd begun the day at 3:00 AM, catching a subway from downtown Toronto to the end of the line, then a bus to Toronto's Pearson Airport for a Toronto-Chicago flight that left at 8:32 AM. It took an hour to get through customs at the airport—an hour of worrying whether he would get through customs. Grandpa's lawyer had suggested he clean himself up a bit before he crossed the border. Webb had done the best he could.

He'd probably checked his passport a hundred times as he shuffled forward in the line. It was a new passport—at least new to Webb. The date of issue was three years earlier. Someone had applied for the passport on his behalf, before Webb had been old enough to do it for himself. And it meant that after the passport had arrived, that same someone had held on to it.

Had his mother applied for it? Or his grandpa?

He couldn't ask his mother; they hadn't spoken in months.

And, of course, he couldn't ask his grandpa. The passport had been in the envelope given to him at the reading of his grandpa's will. Along with the small key, some prepaid bank cards and a letter to Webb from his grandpa, which didn't have much information and nothing at all about the passport. Not much to go on for a trip to the desert.

When he'd reached the front of the line, a middle-aged US Customs and Immigration guy had given Webb's passport a bored look and asked about the purpose of Webb's visit to the States.

"To deliver something for my grandfather," Webb had answered honestly.

"What?"

Webb showed him the key. The customs guy had cocked his head, puzzled.

"I don't know why," Webb answered before the question could be asked. "Before he died, he arranged for his lawyer to pay for my ticket and give me an address in Phoenix so I could deliver the key."

"Return airfare?"

Webb had nodded.

The guy looked hard at Webb, who was wearing a ball cap, trying to look like an upstanding young man.

"You ever had a drug conviction?"

"No, sir," Webb said. It didn't seem like the time and place to explain that he'd been kicked out of high school for drug possession. But, truthfully, there had been no charges, no conviction.

"I could hassle you," the guy said, tapping Webb's passport, "but what matters most is that you have a return ticket. And I think if you were making up a story, it would be a better one than that. If it was important to a dying man, then I'm not going to stop you."

The guy had given Webb's face a final look, then stamped the passport.

After that, there had been an hour's wait for the flight to Chicago, then a delay of another hour, then the flight, then two hours in Chicago's O'Hare Airport, and finally the flight from Chicago to Phoenix. Anyone who thought travel was exciting would have been cured of the illusion by the end of that trip.

Webb had spent most of his time on the plane listening to old rock music on his iPod, imagining where he'd place his fingers for each new chord.

He hadn't reread the letter from his grandpa. Not even once. He didn't need to have it in front of him at all; he'd memorized every word when he first opened it in a café near the lawyer's office.

Webby, I owe an old friend a favor. You'll find his name and address on the back of this letter. Ticket and passport and bank cards will get you there. Whatever you do for him is no different than helping me. I appreciate it. Here's what you need to learn: buried secrets cause pain.

At the lawyer's office, Webb had wondered what Grandpa had written to his cousins.

That was their business though. This was his. When he read the letter, he'd noted the date and time on the ticket, and realized the flight left the next morning; Devine must have arranged the flight sometime between the funeral and the reading of the will. Webb didn't consider for a moment not getting on the airplane. *Whatever you do for him is no different than helping me.*

It was simple; Webb would have done anything to help his grandpa. If he needed to leave on short notice with unclear instructions, would he do it? Yes. The old man had been special.

That meant he'd do the same for Jake Rundell, who lived in a gated community in the northwest part of greater Phoenix, nearly an hour's drive from the airport.

The taxi had taken Webb through the gates and down the boulevard lined with palm trees.

On one side of the boulevard was a sidewalk. On the other side, a fast-flowing creek with ducks.

In the desert?

Outside his air-conditioned cab, it had been 110 degrees.

Ducks, in the desert?

It hadn't taken Webb long to figure it out. Gated community. Expensive houses. It was like an oasis. An artificial oasis made by piles of money. He glimpsed a golf course beyond the houses.

Whoever he was, Mr. Jake Rundell of 2911 Roy Rogers Road, this friend of his grandpa's, was definitely rich.

And, as it turned out, definitely dead.

PART
TWO

In light of the rising frequency of human/grizzly bear conflicts, the Northwest Territories Department of Fish and Game is advising tourists, hikers and fishermen to take extra precautions and keep alert for bears while traveling this summer.

We advise that people wear noisy little bells on their clothing so as not to startle bears. We also advise everyone to carry pepper spray with them in case of an encounter with a grizzly.

It is also a good idea to watch out for fresh signs of bear activity. Outdoorsmen should recognize the difference between black bear and grizzly bear dung.

Black bear dung is smaller and contains lots of berries and squirrel fur.

Grizzly bear dung has little bells in it and smells like pepper.

(Joke circulating on the Internet)

SIXTEEN

NOW

The helicopter was parked a couple of hundred meters away from the Norman Wells airport building and was far larger than the pretty bubble-topped traffic 'copters Webb was used to seeing in Toronto. Webb always thought traffic 'copters were like smug CEOs in expensive suits, telling their employees what to do but never getting their hands dirty themselves.

This chopper was battered and big and ugly and old. Dull green paint showed through in places where the blue paint had worn off. Maybe it had once been an army chopper, taking soldiers in and out of war zones. Much more honorable than hovering far above the fray and daintily sending in radio reports. Webb didn't know much about choppers but guessed this one could have held at least twenty soldiers.

Today it would be carrying a far lighter load. Five by Webb's count.

The pilot was a little man with a big mustache, wearing a jacket with the name of the aviation company across the back. He'd just stepped into the chopper and started the engine.

Besides the pilot and George, there were two middle-aged men, both with strawberry-blond hair and mustaches. Twins. They also had huge matching backpacks with large flags sewn onto them. They were wearing their backpacks instead of resting them on the ground. Stupid, Webb thought. Those backpacks must weigh a ton. Why not rest while you could?

With the rotor of the chopper beginning to turn and pick up speed, Webb pretended he was holding up his iPod to read something as he snapped a photo of the backpacks.

He was close enough to the airport to be connected to the terminal's Wi-Fi, so he googled the flag, and in less than thirty seconds he learned the flag was German.

It would be great, he thought, if they couldn't speak English. That would be two fewer people he'd have to talk to during the hike.

The sixth person on the tarmac was standing a couple of meters away from the Germans. It was Sylvain, the Norman Wells cop.

He caught Webb glancing at him and walked over.

"Just wanted to be sure you made it," Sylvain said. "Things move quickly in a small-town police unit, and I had to let Brent out a half hour ago. Turns out you can't lock someone up for assaulting his own truck, and I didn't get there early enough to see him attack you. The boys there all swear nothing else happened, so it's your word against theirs."

Sylvain pointed at the helicopter. "But I can relax now, knowing you're going to be out of his reach. By the time you get back to Norman Wells, Brent should be out at a work camp, so unless he decides to track you down in Toronto someday, it looks like you're out of harm's way."

Webb nodded a thank-you and followed the Germans onto the chopper to begin the next stage of his trip.

SEVENTEEN

The sun was behind them as the chopper lifted. The roar was muted, because Webb, like the others in the chopper, was wearing a headset that let him communicate with George.

Within seconds the small town was below them, just a collection of buildings that looked like driftwood that the mighty Mackenzie had spewed onto its banks.

And then they were above the river, passing the man-made islands in the center that held the oil wells that defined Norman Wells.

The chopper headed south and west, crossing the brown muddy waters of the wide Mackenzie.

By this point, the river had already gathered the forces of a dozen other rivers, each of them roiling with sediment carried down from distant mountains.

Webb didn't expect the chopper to land for a while, so he was surprised when it dipped just after crossing the river and hovered above a clearing in the woods.

George's voice came over Webb's headset. "None of you have walked the beginning stages of the Canol Trail, but I understand some of you will be returning to make sure you hike every step."

The two German tourists gave each other high fives, which told Webb that they understood English. That meant he'd have to be rude to ignore them. Which was fine with Webb.

"However," George continued, "it's worth mentioning that below us is Mile One. Here is where the building of the Canol Road and pipeline began and where base camp was established in 1943."

Webb tuned George out and concentrated on a guitar riff in his head.

One of the things that Webb knew about himself was that, except for music, he didn't like to learn by listening. Spoken words moved too slowly for him. He preferred to get his information by reading.

It was faster, and when he needed to remember the information, all he had to do was visualize the words. When information entered his brain through his ears instead of his eyes, it was a lot harder to remember. He had a lot of information stored on his iPod; to his way of thinking, his brain was as big as the Internet. He didn't need George to tell him about the Canol Trail. All he needed to do was hold his iPod in the palm of his hand, and in seconds, he could review all the knowledge he'd collected.

The chopper banked forward and headed south-west toward the Mackenzie Mountains, some 24 kilometers away.

The short stunted spruce of the flat plains of the Mackenzie River became a blur beneath them.

The first portion of the Canol Trail would have been easy to walk, Webb thought. Boring because of the flatness, but not so boring since a moose or bear could appear at any second.

If you wanted to walk all 675 kilometers of north-west Arctic from Norman Wells to Whitehorse— the entire length of the Canol Road—you walked a segment of 80 to 130 kilometers every summer. A chopper took you to your starting point and picked you up at the other end. By cutting the trek down to shorter segments, you could carry enough food to last the week it took to go between the mile markers. Or you could choose to walk the Canol Trail, a shorter portion of the original road.

Webb had no intention of walking any of the other segments.

Once he found what he had been sent to find at Mile 112, he was not coming back to hike the rest of the trail. Last thing he wanted was a return trip to Norman Wells and another encounter with Brent Melrose.

Webb wasn't great at math, but the pilot had told him earlier that they would be traveling at about 160 kilometers an hour. So when the helicopter dipped again about fifteen minutes later, at the approach to the Mackenzie Mountains, it surprised him. They couldn't already be at their destination.

This time, instead of hovering, the chopper landed on a gravel bar between sheer canyon walls near a shallow, fast-moving river. The water was so pure and clear, you could see flashes of fish.

All the noise and vibration stopped.

George unstrapped himself from his seat and opened the side door to the chopper. He pointed above him.

"Make sure you keep your heads down," he said. "The blades haven't stopped moving."

Two minutes later, all of them were on the ground. Webb looked around, blown away by the view. The canyon walls that rose above him were reddish brown. He'd never felt so puny, not even among the massive skyscrapers of downtown Toronto.

There was the sound of rocks tumbling high above them.

"Sheep!" George called out.

All of them looked up to see a pair of white mountain sheep, with little ones behind, edging their way along a path 50 or 60 meters straight up.

Webb pulled his eyes away from the sheep and looked downriver. Huge rocks rose like zombie giants.

He noticed a small piece of pipe, twisted and rusty, running along the river's edge. This was all that remained of the work of thousands upon thousands of men: a pipeline meant to send a precious flow of oil from Norman Wells to Whitehorse, 675 kilometers to the west. Webb thought about what it might have been like to be one of the army of workers who built the pipeline, fighting howling winds and lashing snow in temperatures of minus 50 degrees Celsius.

They wouldn't be going that far though.

Godlin Lakes was at Mile 168. That was near where the chopper was going to leave them. They were going to walk back from there to the old pipeline pump station at Mile 108, just beyond Devil's Pass, where the chopper would pick them up in a week. He'd been told that was almost 100 kilometers and that they'd need to average just over 16 kilometers a day.

When the chopper dropped them at Mile 170, they'd be alone in thousands of square miles of the most remote wilderness that Canada had to offer. If there had been any other way for Webb to get to Devil's Pass except with a group, he would have done it.

It had been tempting to use some of the money to hire a chopper to bring him in and out. Straight to Devil's Pass and back to Norman Wells.

Except that's not what his grandfather had wanted him to do.

EIGHTEEN

Webb jumped at an explosion of noise and move-ment in front of him. Almost immediately, he realized it was a bird.

But the two Germans—Fritz and Wilhelm were their names—began to laugh. Webb couldn't tell them apart by looking at their faces, but Fritz wore black pants and Wilhelm wore navy blue. Webb didn't really care if they wore different pants on a different day. He had no intention of getting to know them.

Wilhelm pointed at Webb and said, "Little bird! Big jump!"

He laughed with a meanness that Webb knew all too well was the laugh of a bully.

Webb ignored it and watched the flight of the bird. It was smaller than a chicken, with brown feathers mottled with white. It stopped briefly and blended in with the rocks. It squawked again, getting closer to Webb.

"Ptarmigan," George explained. "A male. Trying to lure you away from its nest. The hen is somewhere nearby, hunkered down. We'll see lots of these displays as we hike."

"Stupid bird," Fritz said. "Very stupid."

He threw a rock and hit it in the head, slamming it onto its side. The ptarmigan spasmed briefly, then stopped moving.

Fritz and Wilhelm laughed again, but froze instantly as George spun on them, anger obvious on his face.

"What?" said Fritz. "Little bird. Dead bird."

"You treat this land with respect," George said. The top of his head only reached the Germans' shoulders, but there was no fear in his voice. Just anger. "We only kill what we can eat."

"Yah, yah," Fritz said.

"That means," George said, "you killed it. You eat it."

"No, no," Fritz said.

"And to eat it," George said, "you slit the belly and remove the breast meat. We take it with us and cook it over a fire later."

"Not me. You. We pay you to be guide."

"And if you don't skin it and gut it, the helicopter takes you back right now. Think that pilot is going to listen to you or to me? Now pick up that bird, and I'll tell you how it's done."

"Get blood on my hands?"

George kept staring at him. "When you killed it, you got blood on your hands. Now are you going to do it, or go back to Norman Wells?"

The German shrugged and walked over to the dead ptarmigan. He nudged it with his foot to make sure it was dead. Then he picked it up, trying to hold it away from his body.

"Good work," George said. "Now get that fancy knife of yours and slit the bird's belly open."

In the air again twenty minutes later, Webb was once more in awe of the scenery, which had changed and now looked like the surface of the moon. They were flying over the Plains of Abraham, the trail's highest point at more than a kilometer and a half above sea level. The plains were vast and barren, amazing in a sad and desolate way. Webb was glad they wouldn't be hiking through this portion of the trail.

George finally broke the communication silence. "Now approaching Devil's Pass," he said. "You'll see the collection of old buildings and trucks at the pump station. That's our final destination."

The chopper climbed and then threaded its way between the granite peaks that seemed to want to pull them down.

Incredible that it would only take them another half hour by chopper to get to Godlin Lakes, and then a week on foot to make it back to Devil's Pass.

Webb didn't spend much time thinking about that, however. Instead, not for the first time, he wondered what had happened at Devil's Pass.

When the chopper left them at Mile 170, all of them stared at it until it disappeared. The distant *thump-thump-thump* of the engine traveled back to them for a while, reminding Webb how alone they were.

Then, finally, there was only the sound of the wind moving through the trees.

"That's it then," George said. "We've got a ways to go. Let's take photos first, and then get started."

He pointed at the weathered mile marker sign.

Each of them took turns kneeling beside the sign and pointing toward it while George took their pictures.

Goofy, Webb thought. Very goofy. But if he didn't do it, they'd wonder why he was here. So he pasted a grin on his face and knelt beside the sign.

Close to four hundred men had died in the two years it took to build a road from Norman Wells to Whitehorse. That was an average of two men a week. Slipping on ice and falling beneath bulldozers. Getting washed away by fierce currents in water that would freeze you to death within minutes. Tumbling off the sides of cliffs. Just so the road could be advanced one mile marker at a time in some of the most brutal conditions on the planet.

And less than three years after completing it, the government had decided it wasn't worth the effort and expense. Or the blood of all those men.

Now the mile markers were mainly used for photo ops. This said something about mankind, Webb knew, but he wasn't going to put any effort into trying to come up with something profound to say about it.

To him, it was just a stupid waste. Although it might make a good song someday.

George stepped forward along a narrow stretch of ground that might once have been a road.

Webb's journey to Devil's Pass had officially begun.

NINETEEN

Webb stayed at the back of the group. At least twenty steps behind. This way, he wouldn't have to talk to anyone. Happily, Fritz and Wilhelm were directly in front of him, talking with George. Their voices carried to Webb, but he couldn't hear the words.

It didn't matter.

He was concentrating on putting one foot in front of the other. A person could take longer strides on city sidewalks, but this wasn't even close to flat and smooth. The rocks felt slippery, even though they were dry. The trail was uneven and frequently took them off the roadbed because the roadbed had broken away.

He had his iPod and his music. He wasn't worried about running out of power. The solar-powered charger took care of that. But somehow he couldn't bring himself to put in his earbuds.

It wasn't that this land was sacred or anything. *Sacred* was too strong a word. But the mountains were so untouched and the air so crisp and the water that trickled into streams that became rivers that fed the Mackenzie was so pure that it all deserved a respect that did verge on the sacred.

Webb wasn't going to walk through it and disrespect it in any way whatsoever. He wasn't going to tell this land that his puny downloads were worth more of his attention. Out here, he understood why George had insisted that not a single thing be left behind on the trail.

That's why it was a shock to Webb when one of the Germans in front of him tossed an object into the bushes.

And kept walking.

Webb didn't.

He stepped into the shrubs at the side of the trail and found what the guy had tossed out.

It was a large flashlight full of D batteries that weighed about two pounds and was probably as bright as a car's headlight. He could understand why the guy didn't want to carry it, because two pounds was a lot of extra weight in a backpack that already weighed a lot. Plus, it never got dark this time of year, so they didn't need it anyway.

Webb grimaced at the thoughtlessness of the littering. There was plenty of room in his backpack, so he put the flashlight in his backpack and followed the others again.

TWENTY

THEN

On that hot day in Phoenix, the woman who had answered the door at 2911 Roy Rogers Road appeared to be about the same age as Webb's mother. Her brown hair was shoulder length. She had faint laugh lines around her eyes. And a puzzled look on her face. Chances were, Webb guessed, teen-aged guys with long hair didn't knock on this door very often.

She glanced at the taxi that was driving away, then back at Webb. She remained standing in the doorway, an obvious clue that she wasn't prepared to invite him inside.

"I'd like to talk to Mr. Jake Rundell," Webb said. "I have a note from him asking me to stop by. I was given the security code to get in here and told I didn't need to call ahead."

It felt good to be in the shade of the house. In the short walk from the street up to the door, he'd begun panting in the heat.

The woman sagged a little, holding on to the frame of the doorway. She took a breath to steady herself, then spoke slowly. "His funeral was a couple of days ago."

Webb felt himself sag too. Jake Rundell was dead?

If Jake Rundell was dead, now what? Nothing in his grandfather's letter could help him. "You're obviously not selling anything," she said. "Otherwise I'd tell you that this community has strict rules against going door to door. But you came in a taxi."

"Flew in from Toronto," Webb said. "This morning. My grandfather sent me."

"He's too old to travel himself?"

"His funeral was a little over a week ago," Webb said. "At the reading of his will, he left me a note saying he owed Jake Rundell a favor and I was supposed to help."

Webb pulled the small key out of his pocket. "I was given this too."

The woman straightened, as if someone had given her a small electric shock.

"You're Jim Webb?" She stepped back. "Please, come inside. Shut the door behind you."

Webb followed her to the living room. Tiled floors. Leather furniture. A huge sliding glass door at the back that showed the brown mountains in the background.

"I'm Jana Rundell," she said, pointing to a chair for Webb to sit in. "The rest of the family has already flown back to their own homes. I've stayed behind to begin getting the house ready for sale."

She moved to the kitchen, which was on the other side of the counter that divided it from the living room. She returned holding a handwritten note and an envelope.

"Here's what it says," Jana told him, reading from the note. "'When Jim Webb shows up with a key, hand him the envelope.'"

Webb took the envelope and opened it. All that was written on it was another address. He read it out loud and gave Jana a questioning look.

She shook her head. "Doesn't mean anything to me."

"Your father didn't say anything else?" Webb asked.

"My father?"

"Jake."

She laughed. "Jake had his eighty-eighth birthday a month ago. He was my grandfather."

"David McLean was ninety-two," Webb said. "He was my grandfather. My mom is about your age. I keep forgetting not everybody had children as late in life as my grandfather."

"David McLean?" Jana said. "Hang on."

She walked out of the open area into what was probably a bedroom. When she came back she handed Webb a black-and-white picture in a frame.

It showed four young men in air-force uniforms. Webb instantly recognized his own grandfather.

Jana leaned over Webb, pointing. "There's my grandfather, Jake. He talked a lot about David McLean. Said there was nobody like him, ever."

"The other two?" Webb asked.

"Harlowe Gavin and Ray Daley. They look like

brothers, don't they? Twins, almost. Grandpa Jake said that, in training camp, Harlowe would take a duty shift for Ray so that Ray could go into town and chase girls, and the commanding officers couldn't tell the difference."

"Long time ago," Webb said, seeing the life and vitality in the young men's faces. It made him sad all over again, knowing his grandpa was gone.

"World War Two," Jana answered. "But I don't have to tell you that, do I?"

Neither spoke. The air-conditioning unit kicked in and a wave of cool air washed over Webb.

"So—"

"So—"

"You first," Jana said.

"My grandfather sent me here to help Jake," Webb said. "He didn't know that Jake was dying." Webb paused. "Or maybe he did. I know he wanted me here as fast as possible."

"Why?" Jana asked.

"I expected Jake Rundell to tell me," Webb answered. He tossed the key into the air and caught it again, leaving his palm open. "But I guess since he knew the end was coming for him, he left me an address instead."

Both of them stared at the key.

"If it helps," Jana said, "I can drive you there."

TWENTY-ONE

NOW

The Godlin Lakes were near the top of the mountains, right alongside the road. A floatplane was tied near a dock on the lake. As the group walked toward the water, Webb saw the wires that were strung from fenceposts surrounding some small cabins. After hiking through vistas straight from a wilderness slide show, finding this collection of shacks felt like stumbling upon civilization.

The two Germans were leading the group, and Fritz, the one who had thrown the flashlight into the bushes, reached the fence first.

"You might not want to do that," George said as Fritz put his hand on the wire to push it down and step over it. Fritz fell backward with a scream, shouting something in German that Webb couldn't understand. It didn't sound good.

When Fritz got up, there was a dark stain at his crotch.

He screamed again, this time at George.

"What is this? What is this?" He pointed at the fence. "You tell me ahead of time, yes? Not wait until it bites me!"

"Bites you?" George asked.

"Shock! Shock! Yes, bites my hand."

George said calmly, "It's why I said you might not want to do that. It's electric. Up there, attached to some batteries from a tractor. That would give anybody a big shock."

"Electric?" Fritz was furious. He pointed at his crotch. "You make me wet my pants."

"Not me," George said. "It's important to listen to your guide out here. Got it?"

The German gave him a dark look but said nothing more.

"Why electric?" Webb asked.

"Bear fence," George said. "Electricity keeps them on the outside. That's a good thing. Tonight we can set up our tents inside."

The commotion had drawn a man from the cabins. He waved and grinned. Since barely two dozen hikers went down the Canol Trail in any summer, Webb guessed that not many visitors came up to the lakes.

"Let me disconnect the electricity," the man called out. "Then you can join me in the big cabin."

While he knew he'd have to join the group for dinner, Webb didn't want to socialize. He just wanted to have time alone to play guitar. At least, for now, he wouldn't have to worry about bears.

"Left here by the army," said Chuck, the man who had waved them into the enclosure. He pointed at a big woodstove inside the main cabin. "Still works good, don't it? I'm a small outfitter. Would have cost me a fortune to get something like this up here."

The fire was crackling, and heavy iron pans on top of the stove were filled with fresh-caught fish and the ptarmigan that Fritz had killed earlier. Some kind of bread was baking on the stove top.

Webb realized he had never been this hungry in his life, not even in the first two weeks after he left home and he'd been eating out of Dumpsters.

Even though his mouth was watering, he waited until George offered him a plateful of fish. Their eyes met.

"You could probably make a little money," George said. "Right here, right now. Lighten your load. Sell some stuff to Chuck. You heard him say how expensive it is to bring things in. I'd bet a lot of your stuff is valuable."

George winked.

Webb remembered how George had made such a big deal about carrying everything out. "You have eyes in the back of your head?" Webb asked.

"Yup," George said.

George turned to Chuck. "See this skinny kid right here, stupid enough to carry a guitar on his pack?"

"Wasn't going to say anything about it," Chuck answered. "But stupid is as stupid does."

The two Germans were busy eating. And watching.

"Well," George said, "this kid's backpack is getting heavy. He has a bunch of stuff he'd be willing to sell you dirt cheap, if you can use it."

"That true?" Chuck asked.

"It is weighing me down," Webb said. He went to the corner of the cabin where he'd set down his backpack. He brought it back and opened the top flap. He pulled out the heavy flashlight that the Germans had thrown out, and set it on the table.

"Could use that," Chuck said. "And if you were idiot enough to bring it out here, I'll be idiot enough to give you a dollar for it."

"It's a twenty-dollar item," Webb said. "The price tag is still on it."

Which was true. It came from The Northern, in Norman Wells.

"Either take my offer or carry it," Chuck said. "Nobody worth anything just throws stuff on a trail out here."

"Sold then," Webb told him. "I don't want to carry it."

Webb pulled out some cans of bear spray.

Chuck laughed. "Pepper spray? Didn't you see the sign on the wall?"

He pointed. The sign explained the difference between black bear droppings and grizzly bear droppings: grizzly bear droppings smelled like pepper. There was an official insignia on the poster, but Webb guessed—and hoped—the poster was meant as a joke.

Chuck continued. "Pepper spray is just going to irritate a grizzly. You don't want be around one when it's not irritated, and you really don't want to be responsible for irritating it. You'll notice George has a rifle. That's what it takes to stop a bear. Three times in the last month, I've had to shoot over a bear's head to get it away from the horses."

Webb pulled out a mini-stove with a butane tank. He'd seen it at The Northern for over a hundred dollars. A solar shower bag was next—fill it with water, and the sun would heat it and you'd have a great outdoor shower. For about thirty bucks.

All of these, of course, Webb had picked up as the Germans dropped each item along the trail. Folding shovel, a set of walkie-talkies, a pair of bright yellow binoculars, and even a stainless-steel mirror.

"Twenty dollars for all of it," Chuck said.

"Except the mirror," Webb said. "I heard some-where a mirror is better than flares for signaling an airplane if you get lost."

"You're smart enough to know that yet dumb enough to carry all that extra gear? Twenty dollars, then, for all of it except the mirror."

The Germans watched, their mouths gaping in surprise. Either because Webb had picked everything up behind them, or because Chuck was offering only twenty dollars.

"Any idea what you have to pay for this in a store?" Webb asked, hiding a smile.

"Any idea how much work it's going to be to take it back to the store, even if you still have your receipts?"

"Lots," Webb said.

"Stupid is as stupid does," Chuck said again. "I've changed my mind. I'll give you fifteen for all of it."

"That is over three hundred dollars of stuff, yes?" Wilhelm squawked.

Webb noticed they didn't want to claim any of it. Maybe they were embarrassed by what they'd done, but Webb doubted it.

"Ten dollars," Chuck said to Webb. "My final offer. Keep in mind, my garbage cans are full already and I have to fly everything out that won't burn."

"Ten dollars then," Webb said. "Good enough for me."

He felt the Germans' eyes on him. He didn't care what they thought. It had been a pain to pick up after them all day. And this was way better than going to George and tattling about it.

"Don't you feel better, kid?" George asked.

"Much," Webb said.

"That guitar must weigh some," Chuck said. "Might give you close to what it's worth."

"Don't go there," George told Chuck. "Threaten to take away the kid's guitar and a real strange light appears in his eyes."

TWENTY-TWO

The night was brief—and cold. It didn't even get dark enough at any point to see stars.

Webb woke up warm, though, loving the down-filled sleeping bag that had taken such a big chunk out of his bank card.

He stepped outside. George was already at a fire, squatting in front of it, warming his hands, a pot of coffee on a grill.

Webb reached into his backpack for his lightweight plastic mug. He picked up a pail and walked with it to the nearby creek, where he filled it, carried it back to the fire and set it beside George.

"Let me guess," George said. "Water to refill the coffee pot?"

Webb nodded.

"Kid, someone raised you right."

Dad was there only until I was ten, Webb thought. And then his mom carried on.

"Just want to treat people the way I'd like to be treated," Webb said.

"You'd think that wouldn't be too much to ask, wouldn't you?" George said.

"You'd think," Webb agreed. In his mind, he saw a flash of a broken broom handle coming down on the soles of his feet. Nothing he could do about those memories. And certainly there was nothing to tell anyone, ever.

George poured coffee into Webb's plastic mug. "Have some before the others wake up. But don't thank me for it. All I'm doing is what I'd expect others to do for me." He grinned.

Webb wrapped his hands around the mug. The ground was wet, and the air was cold enough that he could see his breath.

"That stuff about bears that Chuck told us last night. Is it true? Pepper spray won't stop them?"

"Would you want to take that chance?" George said.

"I know how to shoot pepper spray," Webb said. "But not a rifle."

George grunted. "Let me show you."

He lifted his rifle and explained the safety and showed how to put a bullet in the chamber. "If a grizzly is charging," he said, "shoot as early as you can. They can move as fast as a freight train, and you want as much time as possible to get another bullet in the chamber. Got it?"

"Got it."

George handed Webb the rifle. "Keep the barrel facing the ground. Never, ever point at anything unless you intend to shoot it."

"Got it."

"Safety on?"

"Yes," Webb said.

"Did you check it?"

"No. I saw—"

"Check it yourself. Always."

Webb checked. "On."

"Good. I'm going to set up a target."

Leaving Webb with the rifle, George moved about thirty steps away to prop up three pieces of wood like a tripod. He returned to Webb.

"Good," he repeated. "I like that you kept the barrel down."

"The target's pretty close, isn't it?" Webb asked.

"I don't need to teach you to shoot like a sniper. Just how to shoot and keep the rifle steady and get the confidence to hit a nearby target. We aren't here to hunt grizzlies, but we need to be able to defend ourselves if one gets close. Now hold the butt of the rifle snug against your shoulder. It's going to kick when you fire, and if you leave a gap, it will feel like a mule kicked you."

Webb lifted the rifle.

"Get the bead at the front between the notches of the sight and line them up with the target. Squeeze the trigger, don't pull."

Webb took a breath. Squeezed the trigger. Heard nothing but a *click*.

"Too bad," George said. "The charging grizzly just ripped off your scalp."

"Safety," Webb said. "I forgot."

He snapped the safety off. Aimed again. Squeezed the trigger.

It felt like someone had punched him in the shoulder. The explosion echoed and re-echoed.

"Not worried about waking the others?" Webb asked.

"Wanted to pour cold water on them while they were sleeping," George said. "I don't take lightly to people who litter the trail. I'm more worried about you actually hitting a piece of wood. Try again."

It took three shots for Webb to hit one of the pieces of wood. It popped up and landed a couple of steps farther away. The other two pieces fell from the tripod, and with his next two shots, he hit first one, then the other, scattering them.

"Good," George said. "Looks like you got it figured out. If we see a grizzly, you tell me if you think you can handle the warning shots."

He put the rifle away just as the Germans appeared. George waved them away. "Nothing to panic about. Pack up, we're hitting the trail in twenty minutes."

Fritz and Wilhelm disappeared again.

Webb and George spent a few minutes in friendly silence, sipping their coffee.

"Storm's coming in," George said. "You'll be glad you have good rain gear."

"You telling me that so I'll know you went through my backpack at some point?"

"I went through everybody's backpack. Right after the pilot loaded them on the chopper. I'm responsible for all of us. No drugs or alcohol allowed."

"And since I'm a skinny kid with long hair and a guitar, you thought you'd find drugs."

Good thing, Webb thought, that George didn't know why Webb left high school. Good thing it wasn't on his record. He would have been unable to cross the border to go to Phoenix.

"Crossed my mind," George answered. "Especially since you don't seem like the type who goes looking for outdoor adventures. But if you don't want people thinking that about you, cut your hair and find another T-shirt. People take you as they find you. Until they learn different. Heard Brent Melrose learned different."

There was nothing to say to that, so Webb just watched the approaching storm.

"Those Germans were mad when they found out I left their expensive Scotch behind in Norman Wells," George said. "They each had a bottle. I wasn't worried about the excess gear though. I thought they'd at least be able to make it to Godlin Lakes before deciding it wasn't worth carrying. Chuck, he loves all the good deals I bring him with each new group. I told him that you'd been picking up after those two, and he nearly peed himself laughing."

"The fence thing," Webb said. "Not an accident."

"Not an accident. A person's got to treat this land right. I nearly pulled your iPod out back in Norman Wells but figured I'd give you a chance not to listen to it."

"Nearly did," Webb said. "But there's something about this land."

George looked at him. "I'll tell you this. Last night I understood what it is with you and that guitar. What you played sounded like it came straight down from the sky and mountains. It was music touched by the spirits."

Webb hadn't felt like ramping it up when he'd wandered away in the twilight to be by himself with his guitar. That's what the sky and mountains did to a person.

"Sorry," Webb said. "Next time I'll go a little farther from camp. I should have figured sound would carry out here."

"It wasn't like that at all," George said. "What I heard made me walk out a little farther so I could hear it better. Your grandfather was right. He told me you were an amazing musician."

"You spoke to my grandfather!" This was a surprise to Webb. He'd expected George at the Norman Wells airport, but only because of the instructions he'd been given by letter. It had never occurred to him that George and his grandpa had ever had a conversation.

"I did," George said. "He wanted to know more about the Canol Trail and what it might be like for you. He asked a lot of questions. He said he had plans to send you out to find something and that someday I would hear from you. I enjoyed my conversation with him. He sounded like a remarkable man."

"Yes," Webb said. "He was."

"Two things he wanted me to pass along to you when the time was right," George said. "This feels like it's right."

Webb waited.

"The first he said you already knew: *That which does not kill us makes us stronger.*"

"Nietzsche. Frederick Nietzsche. A German philosopher." Webb had looked him up online.

"Your grandfather said the two things he wanted to pass along came from that man," George said. "The first thing, yes, very wise. I think about this, the land. The longer you survive it, the stronger you become. But the second thing? I don't know how it matters on the Canol Trail."

George closed his eyes and Webb could see that he was making sure to tell him word for word what his grandfather wanted to pass along. "*He who fights with monsters might take care lest he thereby become a monster. And if you gaze for long into an abyss, the abyss gazes also into you.*"

George opened his eyes and nodded. "Yes, that was it. All of it. That make sense to you?"

Webb shook his head. "Not at all."

"Me neither," George said. He shrugged. "Next time you play guitar at night, you join us at the fire, okay?"

TWENTY-THREE

"Hey, guitar boy. Yes. You."

Fritz. Or maybe Wilhelm. Webb couldn't tell since they were walking up behind him. Webb was sitting on a rock overlooking the valley ahead. The distant hill was dotted with caribou.

Webb stood and faced them and spoke. "No speak English."

"Yes," Fritz said. "Very funny."

"Yes, funny, like how you sell our equipment last night," Wilhelm said. They kept their shoulders close together, gaining strength from each other. "Give us the money."

Webb couldn't see George anywhere nearby. Not that it mattered, much.

"Sure," Webb said. He had the ten-dollar bill in his pocket. "It's yours. Every penny I got for all of it."

They looked disappointed, like they were hoping he would put up more of a fight. That made it worthwhile to Webb—disappointing them.

"Not enough," Wilhelm said.

"Tell that to the cowboy," Webb answered. "I did the best I could to get more money from him."

"Not enough," Fritz said.

They moved closer, as if Webb's refusal to put up a fight made them bolder. Proving Webb right: they were bullies.

For Webb, it was just like another street situation. Sometimes you ran. Sometimes you fought. You made the choice based on what was best for your survival, not what was best for your pride.

"We'll make you pay," Wilhelm said.

Webb was okay with running if he had to. But running here would only delay what Fritz and Wilhelm really wanted, which was blood. Sooner or later, they'd force Webb to fight. No sense waiting and wondering and looking over his shoulder during the next week.

As Webb stood, he palmed a rock about the size of a baseball.

The Germans took another collective step, which was enough to convince Webb his guess was correct. They weren't trying to scare him; they wanted to hurt him.

He showed them the rock.

"We're close enough," Webb said, "that if I throw this, I'm not going to miss. And we're close enough that one of you will be hurt really badly."

Webb didn't feel anger like this very often. A couple of days earlier, he'd been ready to drive over Brent in his own truck. And once in high school, a bigger kid had tried pushing him around in the hallway, mocking him for the military haircut he had been forced to get when Elliott made him sign up for junior cadets. Without warning, Webb had viciously punched the kid in the stomach, then pulled him to the ground by his hair and knelt with his knee on the kid's throat, promising to crush the kid's windpipe if he messed with him again. Webb had been as surprised by his response as the bigger kid had been.

It had definitely been an overreaction. Thinking about it later, Webb realized that the kid in the hallway had been a convenient scapegoat for his anger at his stepfather.

Whatever the reason—and he didn't spend too much time analyzing it—Webb had learned a couple of things. First, he was a lot tougher than he realized he was; he knew *that which does not kill us makes us stronger* was true. And second, responding with a tremendous overreaction made people think you were nuts, so they didn't mess with you. It was something he'd learned subconsciously from Elliott. *Choose your guitar over obedience to me, and your mother will pay the price.*

Webb had also learned from Elliott that a soft-voiced psycho was very intimidating.

"Are you prepared to kill me?" Webb asked mildly. "Do you understand? Kill me? Because that means you will go to jail for a long time, understand?"

"Not kill," Wilhelm said quickly. "Just hurt."

"No," Webb said. "If you try anything, you better kill me. Otherwise, when you're asleep, I'll sneak into your tent and slit you open like that ptarmigan yesterday. You see, I don't care if I go to jail. And I'll be happy to kill you anytime. Because in case you haven't figured it out, I'm not normal."

He braced himself, ready to fire the rock into Fritz's skull, but he held himself in control. Just barely.

"So ask yourself," he said, looking from one to the other. He could hear Elliott's voice echoing in his own memories as he spoke. "Am I bluffing? Or will I hit one of you so hard they'll have to fly you to a hospital?"

"No bluff," Wilhelm said, putting up his hands. "You leave us alone. We leave you alone."

"Good decision," Webb said. He dropped the rock at his feet and smiled coldly as they backed away.

He hated himself for that cold smile.

TWENTY-FOUR

The storm hit hard halfway through the second day and caught them at Mile 152. Everyone threw on rain gear and kept slogging. What else was there to do? They made it to Mile 147 before George signaled they should stop for the night.

Putting up tents in the rain with cold, soaked fingers was a pain. Webb didn't complain though. He saw no point in it. Besides, he'd faced worse when he was actually living on the streets, before he'd figured out how to make enough money to pay rent at a cheap boardinghouse.

Lighting a fire was easier than he expected.

George carried chemical fire-starter paste, and even though the twigs they collected for kindling were wet on the outside, they snapped with a satisfying noise that indicated they were dry on the inside.

Webb helped George build the fire, starting with the twigs and adding thicker and thicker pieces of wood until it was roaring.

That night, Webb didn't wander away to play his guitar. Once his hands were warm from the fire, and after eating some noodles, he slipped into his tent and strummed there.

He played without thinking, losing himself in the music as he always did. It was necessary to play. Because it kept away the thoughts of the pain that he'd inflicted on his mother.

It had been raining for twenty-four hours nonstop when the group came to a stream at the bottom of a narrow valley. Black silty water rushed through the gorge.

Webb heard a sound he couldn't recognize. An occasional deep cracking sound.

He asked George what it was.

"Rocks," George answered, his face grim. "Tumbling through the water. A man falls in there, he doesn't stop rolling until he washes into a river a couple of hours downstream. And that river will be so full, it will have standing waves."

George asked all of them to wait while he walked upstream along the stream, looking for higher ground. He returned about ten minutes later, wordlessly shook his head, and then walked downstream.

When he came back, he said, "There is a spot. But we'll have to rope our way across. I'll need the extra I asked you to carry in your guitar case."

Webb grinned. "Yup. One thing that never hurts out here. Rope."

George led them to a place where they could walk down an angled gravel bar to a spot that was only about six feet across the water from some trees on the other side.

George took out a bundle of rope from his backpack and knotted one end to the rope from Webb to double the length.

Mercifully, the rain had died down to a drizzle, and the air seemed to be getting warmer.

"First guy has it toughest," George said. "Would be better if two went across together."

Webb nodded. Neither of the Germans moved.

George pointed at Fritz. "You wanted adventure. Here it is."

George put a hand on Webb's shoulder. "This will be a piece of cake."

Webb nodded.

George tied the rope first around Webb's chest and then around Fritz's chest, leaving lots of slack between them. With the rest of the length of the rope in his hands, he went to a tree and wrapped the other end around the trunk.

"If you fall, Wilhelm and I will haul you back. When you get to the other side, wrap the rope around a tree trunk and we'll use it as a bridge to go across."

The water was only knee deep but moving so fast that as Webb and Fritz stepped into it, it boiled up above their waists. They linked arms and braced themselves, facing upward against the water.

A rolling rock banged into Webb's shin. He grunted with pain.

"We can do this," Webb shouted above the roaring of the water. "No turning back."

Inch by inch, they fought the current, with Webb first, closest to the other side.

It became too deep to continue. The tree trunks were agonizingly close but still out of reach.

"Can't go farther," Fritz shouted back. "Will fall."

Webb had a vision of the two of them being swept downstream, and of the other two on the gravel bar, straining to hold on to the rope.

"Let go of me then," Webb shouted. "I'm going to jump for it."

"Guitar boy, you crazy?"

"No other choice."

Webb eyed the tree that was his target. It was a little downstream. He figured that once he jumped, the water would sweep him toward it.

Without giving himself time to think about how scared he was, he pushed off and fell forward in an awkward dive, reaching out with his arms.

There!

He caught the tree trunk—barely, even as the water tried to sweep his lower body farther down the stream.

But the water wasn't going to win. It took only a second or two to pull himself out of the water and find the shore with his feet.

The rope was straining hard.

Fritz had lost his footing and was flopping around in the middle of the stream, his head barely above water.

"Give us some slack!" Webb shouted across to George.

George understood Webb's intentions. He reeled out some rope, and the momentum of the water swung Fritz toward Webb. He managed to get a hand on Fritz's jacket and clawed until he had a good grip, then pulled Fritz to safety.

Fritz grinned, his face spattered with the dark silt that the water carried. "Thanks. I owe you."

"Yup," Webb said. "I'd say ten dollars is about the right amount."

TWENTY-FIVE

THEN

Jana Rundell backed the Lexus convertible out of the garage at 2911 Roy Rogers Road in Phoenix, with the top down and Webb in the passenger seat.

Jana was so close to his own mother in age, that it struck Webb that in a different life, one where he didn't have a stepfather who knew how to hurt people without leaving a mark, this could have been an ordinary day driving with his mother. But ordinary days had been taken away from Webb the day his mother married again, and there was nothing he could do about it, except block it out of his thoughts and feelings.

He forced himself not to think about what he'd left behind in Toronto, and concentrated on the desert scenery as they drove. The dull brown mountains shimmered in the heat. Palm fronds flashed above them as they moved down the boulevard and out of the oasis of the gated community.

They drove through the desert for a while on a long stretch of black asphalt, the occasional cactus looking like a lonely soldier, until they reached another community, where Jana used the GPS to navigate through an industrial area to a storage place that advertised air-conditioned units.

"I thought the number was an apartment," Jana said, "but I guess it's not."

Webb read from the piece of paper left for him by Jake Rundell. "Five-oh-three."

Jana drove the Lexus up and down the narrow alleys between the storage units until she found it.

Webb stepped out of the car, conscious of the heat. Jana stayed behind the steering wheel.

Finally, the key in Webb's hand made sense. It fit the lock of storage unit 503. The lock opened, allowing him to slide a lever open. He lifted the storage unit door, and it rattled upward loudly.

Cool air wafted toward Webb from the dark interior. There was enough sunlight, however, to show something large and white at the end of the storage unit.

He blinked, and then it made sense. It was a portable movie screen.

"There's a light switch," Jana said.

Because of the intensity of his curiosity, he hadn't realized she'd come into the unit.

"If this isn't my business," she said, flipping on the light, "tell me, and I'll go back and sit in the car."

Centered in front of them was a small table with a projector that faced the movie screen. There was a chair on each side.

"Two chairs," Webb said. "If your grandfather set this up, he wasn't expecting just me."

"Thank you," she said quietly.

They moved inside.

On the table beside the projector was a large sealed envelope with a note paper-clipped to it: *Watch the movie first. Then open the envelope.*

Webb handed Jana the note.

"My grandfather's handwriting," she said.

"They must have planned this together," Webb told her. "Your grandfather and mine."

"Why not just tell you?" she asked.

"I guess we're about to find out," Webb said, pointing at the projector.

She laughed softly. "I wondered where it had gone. We made so much fun of it when Grandpa was alive."

Webb didn't interrupt, because she was crying as she laughed.

"Grandpa Jake took tons and tons of home movies when my mom was little," Jana said. "Home movies, not home video. That was in the sixties. Grandpa Jake showed me his movie camera once. He was so proud of it. A Kodak Brownie that shot eight-millimeter film. You had to use a key to wind it."

She wiped her face. "Every Christmas, he'd set up the movie screen and this projector. Look at it."

It had two huge film reels. A full one at the front and an empty take-up reel at the back.

"Half the time, the film would snap or it would get caught up in the teeth, and it would take him an hour to get it going again. He'd taken movies of the kids diving in the pool. He'd run it in reverse so that it looked like they were jumping backward out of the water and landing on the diving board. We never got tired of watching it and laughing about it."

Webb thought of the video of his grandpa that he'd seen in Devine's law office. He doubted Jake Rundell had done the same, using instead technology that was more than half a century old.

"I'll pull the door back down most of the way," Webb said. "That will make it dark enough to see what he wanted us to see."

The door rattled again, and Webb left a small gap at the bottom, just enough so he'd be able to reach under and pull it open again when the movie was finished.

Jana hit the switch on the projector and the reels clattered into motion. As the opening image hit the screen, Webb turned off the light.

He made his way to the chair on the right side of the projector and sat to watch.

TWENTY-SIX

NOW

"Crap," Webb said. And meant it. He pointed at the pile near his feet.

They were walking up the incline toward the summit of Devil's Pass, just beyond Mile 116. Walking was easy because the trail had plenty of gravel. It felt soft and springy because of all the rain that had fallen on the previous day. Here, unlike many parts of the Canol Trail, it was obvious there had once been a road.

The trail also had plenty of something else.

"Impressive," George said, stopping to examine what Webb had pointed out. "I don't see any little bells in it, and it doesn't smell like pepper. Must mean the grizzly hasn't eaten any hikers lately."

"Ha, ha," Webb said.

George unstrapped his rifle. The *click* as he took it off safety sounded like the bang of a drum.

"What is this?" Fritz said, his voice more high-pitched than normal.

For the first time, Webb felt sympathy for the man. Webb was plenty scared himself. The only reason he hadn't said anything was because his throat was too tight.

It was obvious why George had unstrapped the rifle. The pile of grizzly dung was so wet that it gleamed in the sunlight, and flies were all over it. The rocks beside it had already dried from the rainfall, so that could only mean the dung was very, very fresh.

And very, very large. Webb doubted he could manage an output like that in an entire week.

"What is this?" Fritz repeated. He stepped backward, with Wilhelm clutching his arm.

George waved him into silence and pointed at the ground just a little farther ahead.

Webb's throat, if possible, became even tighter. There was a set of paw prints, where the weight of a heavy animal had pressed down into the soft gravel. The prints were deep enough to hold water. And the prints still held water.

Which meant that the heavy animal responsible for those prints—and the big pile of droppings— had been here very recently.

"Don't move," George said.

Webb looked up the trail and saw it.

The grizzly.

George spoke in a low voice to Webb. "You ready to take the rifle?"

"What?" Webb whispered.

"You had plenty of practice the other day," George said in a low voice. "Take this rifle, and if I tell you, shoot over the bear. If you need to, you can always give me back the rifle."

That which does not kill us makes us stronger.

Webb took the rifle. He could feel his heartbeat throbbing in the side of his neck. He sighted down the rifle at the grizzly.

It stared back.

It stood, waving its massive paws like it was swatting flies. It looked like it filled the road.

Webb kept his finger on the trigger but didn't pull. He had the sights of the rifle on a patch of white fur just below the bear's shoulders.

"Now," George said. "Shoot over its head."

Webb lifted the sights and pulled the trigger. The rifle thundered, and the bear almost fell backward, then bolted down the path, scattering gravel behind it.

Webb put the safety back on and handed the rifle to George.

"Good job," George said. "Feel stronger now?"

"That was more than difficult. What if I had frozen?"

"There would have been enough time for me to take the rifle from you. But I knew you could do it. Your grandfather told me you were strong. He asked me to look for a chance to let you prove it to yourself."

In his tent, Webb couldn't sleep. He'd earned George's trust and didn't take it lightly.

George reminded Webb of his grandfather. A solid man. Unafraid of adventure. Or danger.

Webb missed his grandfather so badly that he wanted to wake George up and talk again, simply because it would feel like talking to his grandfather. Webb didn't hate that grampa had died. He remembered what his he had said in his final video message: *I don't want you to be too sad. I had a good life.*

Webb did hate that he'd had to keep secrets from his grandfather. Not minor secrets like all kids kept from their parents, but something as big as the fact that his stepfather beat him without leaving a mark and had threatened to hurt Webb's mom if he said anything about it.

Webb wondered if telling George about it would ease the burden. But what if George decided to tell Sylvain, and Sylvain reported it to the authorities in Toronto? Then the secret would truly be exposed, and Webb's mom would pay the price.

Besides, then George would learn why Webb had been kicked out of high school.

Thinking about that day, Webb remembered most clearly the ticking of the clock in the hallway at school.

It was 9:26. Fifteen minutes before the next bell would ring and kids would pour out of their classes.

Mid-September, and Webb was two days past his seventeenth birthday. He was taller than Elliott now. He didn't need a mirror to confirm it; he was looking over Elliott's crew-cut hair as Mrs. Gaukel, the principal, fumbled to unlock Webb's locker. Elliot had signed a permission form allowing the search.

It was just the three of them, and it was so quiet he could hear the principal's asthmatic breathing. The locker clicked open.

"Mr. Skinner," she said. "I really don't believe what the anonymous letter said, so I apologize for this. Jim is one of our best students. All you need to do is look at him. You can tell he's going to follow in your footsteps."

Webb understood what she was talking about. Webb's crew cut matched Elliott's for precision. His blue jeans were ironed, for crying out loud. All the friends he used to argue with about the Rolling Stones were no longer friends. Webb didn't have friends. Didn't want friends.

Two years as a junior cadet and Webb was iron-tough. He had height but no bulk. Muscle, and no fat.

He ran four miles at an average pace of five minutes, thirty-two seconds. But no matter how tough cadets' training made him, he still wept silently whenever Elliott hurt him. Webb didn't dare let his mom hear him cry.

"I'm glad you called me here for this," Elliott said. "False accusations are a horrible thing."

Webb saw the irony in that and had no doubt that Elliott intended it for him. Nobody knew the real Elliott. Except Webb. If Webb accused Elliott of abuse, if would just look like a false accusation. And then his mother would pay the price.

Principal Gaukel took Webb's backpack down from a hook inside the locker. She gave an apologetic shrug and unzipped the front pocket. Principal Gaukel tugged at the edge of a baggie that protruded from the open pocket. It could have been a sandwich bag, except it didn't hold a sandwich.

She gasped. "No."

Elliott took the bag and opened it. The unmistakable smell of marijuana bloomed from the baggie.

"Apparently," Elliott said in his silky voice, "the accusation wasn't false after all."

He handed the baggie back to Principal Gaukel and said, "I think you and I should have a discussion in the office. But in the meantime, I'd like a few minutes alone with Jim here."

"Certainly," she said. She looked at Webb. "Jim, I'm disappointed."

Principal Gaukel walked away.

The clock showed 9:28. In less than two minutes, Webb's life had shifted as drastically as if an earthquake had hit the school.

"Drugs," Elliott said.

"Apparently," Webb said, "the accusation wasn't false after all."

Elliott shook his head. "You don't think I've heard about the martial-arts training you've taken at cadets? About all the hours and hours you've worked at it? The instructor tells me that you're one of the best he's seen."

Webb kept his gaze on Elliott's eyes. Training was easy. All he had to do was think about the day that he would beat the crap out of Elliott. A day that got closer with every new move that Webb learned and practiced and conquered.

"You're wondering whether you can take me," Elliott said. "Don't try. There are things you really don't want to learn. Things that make what you've already learned seem like a day at the spa. So maybe you shouldn't come home tonight. I'll tell Charlotte about this myself."

"Maybe I'll tell her."

"Maybe not. All along, I've told you I want her to be happy. You've just proven she is better off without you in her life. So you walk. And I win. The war is over. Don't talk to her. Unless you don't want her to be happy."

For far too long, Webb had lived with the belief that someday Elliott might hurt his mother. Was it because Elliott's veiled threats were perfectly worded? Or was it because after losing his dad, Webb's guilt of not saving his dad and his hidden fear of another loss had never slipped away? Did his mother need protection? Or was the horrible blackness of confusion simply an enemy Webb could never conquer? Webb was too afraid to push for the answer.

He didn't go home. Or speak to his mother again. Not even at the funeral or the reading of the will. He'd lived on the streets for the next two weeks after getting caught with the bag in his locker—diving in Dumpsters for food, pushing past boarded-up windows to sleep in abandoned buildings, washing up in the bathroom at Tim Hortons. Things got a bit better when he got the guitar and the dish-washing job. He was always lonely, but he believed that by enduring this loneliness, he could keep his mother safe.

TWENTY-SEVEN

Sitting in his sleeping bag that night, Webb snapped a nylon string on his guitar as he was quietly strumming inside the tent. He hadn't been focused on any particular riff. Instead, he'd just been humming to the notes, thinking through what he had to do early in the morning to fulfill the quest that he'd been sent to accomplish.

The snapped guitar string didn't irritate him. He'd brought extra nylon and steel strings. He removed the broken string. But force of habit wouldn't let him discard it. Instead, he reached for his pants, which were folded neatly beside the bed. Sleeping in clothes inside a sleeping bag wasn't a good idea. Clothes were never completely dry and the dampness would chill him. Webb wound the length of nylon string into a circle and slipped it into the front pocket of his pants, then folded them again and set them nearby for when he woke up in the morning. Later, he'd burn the nylon in a campfire. He'd done that once already on this trip, feeding the nylon slowly into it like a snake, watching the flame burn the nylon like it was the wick of a candle.

He took another drink of water from the bottle beside him, knowing what it would do to him. Then he rested on his side, waiting to fall asleep.

Sure enough, he woke up a couple of hours earlier than usual. The water had worked as well as any alarm clock.

He slid out of his sleeping bag, wishing he could enjoy the warmth and go back to sleep. But he didn't know if there would be a better chance to do what he had to do, before everyone else woke up.

Inside the small tent, he fumbled as he pulled on his pants, then his boots. He slipped into his shirt and jacket, and he pushed outside and looked up at a pale blue sky, still amazed at the fact that it was not dark.

No clouds either. The edge of the sun's brightness hung over the horizon, like it always did up here this early in the morning at this time of year.

He checked his watch: 4:00 AM. Light enough to see where he was going. And early enough that everyone else was still snoring in their tents. He'd be back long before anyone woke up, so it was safe to leave his guitar and pack behind.

He tiptoed through the campsite and then sprinted around a corner in the trail, where he stopped to empty his bladder.

Then he headed toward Mile 112.

About fifty meters past Mile 112, there was a natural ravine, with rivulets in the mud from the rain that had fallen in the previous days.

Webb saw it and realized it was exactly what he needed.

He stepped into the mud and walked into the ravine. He looked back and saw with satisfaction that his boot prints were very obvious. He continued to the bottom of the ravine, and as the sides came closer together and the bushes grew denser, he deliberately snapped branches as he pushed his way forward.

He was leaving a clear path.

And for a simple reason.

At the fire the other morning, when George discussed the phone conversation he'd had with Webb's grandfather, George had mentioned that he knew Webb had been sent to find something. The phone conversation had taken place long before Webb had gone to the storage unit in Phoenix, long before Webb had read the letter from Jake Rundell.

Webb wasn't sure if his grandfather knew what Jake had requested, or if his grandfather had sent Webb to Jake simply because Jake needed help. Either way, Webb suspected that what he'd been sent to find was something that needed to stay secret. Since George knew that Webb had been sent to find something, and since there was so little time left before they were to be picked up by helicopter, George could guess that Webb was very close to completing his grandfather's task.

If what he'd been sent to find was something that should remain secret, Webb didn't want to take any chances. His real destination was Mile 112, and he'd be careful not to leave any tracks there when he left the Canol Trail there.

Here, however, it was going to look like he'd gone a long way into the bush, and it would be easy to follow his tracks.

Webb kept snapping branches and leaving heavy footprints where possible, until he reached a stream with a rocky bed. He crossed it and walked another twenty paces, then walked backward in his footprints to the stream.

He washed his boots thoroughly of mud, watching the silt leave trails in the clear water. When he was satisfied there was nothing left on the soles of his boots, he began hopping from rock to rock, going upstream for about fifty meters. Occasionally, he would look back and satisfy himself that he'd left no traces. Finally, he slipped away from the stream, and as carefully as possible, climbed back up to the trail about a hundred meters short of Mile 112. He followed his footprints to the mile marker and saw his earlier tracks continue toward the ravine.

From there, he cut south to follow the instructions in the letter from Jake Rundell.

TWENTY-EIGHT

It was eerie to Webb how well the instructions in Jake's letter matched the terrain.

Go directly south from Mile 112. It will take you down a path toward a split rock, the height of a man. Stay left until you get to the stream. Walk upstream to the first fork. Climb the cliff and look for a pile of rocks at the edge overlooking the river below. The necklace is beneath the rocks. Take the necklace to the address on the piece of paper inside this envelope.

It took Webb five minutes to reach the base of the cliff. A few times along the way, he paused, fighting the sensation that he was being followed. He told himself he was paranoid because of how hard he'd worked to leave a false trail.

It took another ten minutes to navigate his way upward, following a twisting, turning path that looked like a game trail.

At the top, the meter-high pile of rocks was obvious. There could be no doubt that it had been stacked by human hands. It was only about 400 meters off the old Canol Road, but with so few people going down the trail, this pile of rock could have remained undiscovered for decades, if not centuries. Only someone who knew it was there would have had a reason to go to it.

The rocks varied from baseball-sized to basketball-sized. Webb began dismantling the pile carefully, not knowing how far down he'd have to go to find the necklace, not knowing if the necklace was in a metal box or something else that could survive the elements. Something had to be there though. Why else would someone go to the trouble of piling the rocks in such a specific place?

After a while he stopped setting the rocks aside with any degree of care. There were just so many of them. He threw them to one side, not even bothering to see where they landed.

Any minute he expected to see a glint of gold or the shape of a box.

Ten minutes later came the moment of discovery. Followed immediately by confusion.

Whatever it was that was gleaming from between a couple of rocks wasn't a necklace. Not even close.

He pulled away another rock and saw that what he had uncovered was the handle of a knife. Leaving it where it was, he pulled away a few more rocks and saw something that sucked the breath out of him completely.

Ragged bits of faded green cloth covering what looked like bone.

He tossed aside a few more rocks and his fears were confirmed.

The rocks had concealed a human body, its flesh long since consumed by the elements. All that was left was skeletal, partially covered in what was barely recognizable as an army uniform. And the rusted blade of a knife was stuck between the ribs.

This was a burial mound. And judging by the position of the knife, there was no doubt the person had been murdered.

Webb was stunned.

Below the skull, Webb saw what he'd been looking for. Gold chain. Flesh decayed, but gold never tarnished. Attached to the gold chain was a thin heart-shaped ceramic pendant.

Gently, he lifted it over the skull and put it in his front pocket. After a moment, he decided to take the knife as well. He wondered why he was feeling so calm. Maybe because this didn't seem real. But it was real. And he'd have to report the body to Sylvain.

There was a military dog tag around the bones of the neck too. He took it as gently as he'd taken the pendant. The name on the tag was clearly etched, even though so much time had passed, because a military dog tag was meant to be able to identify the soldier for as long a possible.

Harlowe Gavin.

Gavin.

He knew that name.

But another thought distracted Webb. How could his grandfather and Jake have known about the body? Unless one or both of them had put it there.

Was his grandfather a murderer?

Webb made a quick decision to hide the body again. He'd wrestle later with whether to tell anyone about it.

He began to stack the rocks again, covering the body as quickly as he could. He had just set down the final rock, when he heard a scuffle behind him.

He turned, half expecting to see the grizzly again.

There was a blur of motion, and Webb barely had time to register that someone was swinging the butt of a rifle toward his head.

Then came the *flash-bang* of impact again, and Webb fell backward onto the pile of rocks.

TWENTY-NINE

Webb woke, staring into the barrel of a rifle held by a man with a dirty bandage across his nose, and deep, dark bruises around his eyes.

Brent Melrose.

"I've been waiting for an opportunity like this," Brent said, finger on the trigger, aiming down the rifle.

"That's the best you got?" Webb answered. No way was he going to let on that he felt like someone had dumped a bucket of ice water on him. He fought against shivering. This was real. This was scary.

"What?"

"Of course you've been waiting for an oppor-tunity like this. Finding me alone. Otherwise you wouldn't be out here."

If Webb was going to die in the next few seconds, he was not going to give Brent the satis-faction of seeing his fear. Webb had spent too much of his life being afraid. Fear had become such a good friend that he'd learned to embrace it and use it to motivate him. *That which does not kill us makes us stronger.*

Now, however, it looked like Webb wasn't going to have a chance to survive this and become stronger.

"I'd really like to pull this trigger," Brent said. "Especially when you come up with smart-ass stuff like that. But I didn't walk eighty kilometers down the Canol to let you off that easy after everything you've done to me."

He lowered the rifle.

Webb realized his hands and feet were bound with zip ties. At least Brent hadn't thought to tie his hands behind him. Still, the distance between him and Brent was at least a meter. Even if he could somehow lurch to his feet and spring forward, he didn't have a chance of taking Brent by surprise.

Behind Webb was the edge of the cliff overlooking the river. Falling from it probably wouldn't kill him, because there was a lot of bush growing off the sides of it. But no way could Webb jump, fall through the bush, land and hop away with his ankles bound together before Brent either walked to the edge of the cliff and shot him like a fish in a barrel, or made his leisurely way down and recaptured him. Or maybe Brent wouldn't even have to finish him off. The river was swollen and raging from the recent rains. Chances were that Webb's fall would take him into the water.

"She left me, you know," Brent said. "Told me she didn't deserve to be hit." He grinned a horrible grin. "Funny thing is, that's the last thing I heard you say to her at the airport. Guess I know who to blame, don't I? Made me want to kill you even before you broke my nose and made a fool of me. So after you left in the helicopter, I took a boat across the river and drove an ATV as far up the Canol as I could. Had to stop at Dodo Canyon—no machines can make it through there.

Then I started walking. I knew you'd be on the trail headed this way to Mile 108 for the flight back to Norman Wells. All I had to do was get there before you did. Wasn't that hard for me. I was motivated. I really wanted to kill you."

Brent hefted his rifle and pointed it at Webb. The black hole at the end of the barrel was terrifying.

Brent grinned and lowered the rifle. "I was waiting outside your tent, looking for the perfect chance to do something, when you made it easy for me by slipping out when everyone was asleep. From the trail, I could hear you crashing through the bushes down below, and I didn't want to follow because the mud would leave another set of tracks. I was wondering what to do, when I heard you coming back up through the trees. Don't know why you did all that fancy stuff of setting up another trail, but you made this so simple. So there's no proof I was here and no proof I followed you."

Webb didn't like hearing that.

Brent was obviously crazy. If he preferred having Webb tied up and helpless over shooting him, it could only be because he had worse things in mind than a quick bullet to the head. Webb didn't want to imagine what those things could be.

"When I'm finished with you, you can go back to your camp," Brent said. "I don't have to kill you. I'll just disappear for a while. You can say whatever you like, but it will be your word against mine, because no one is going to see me but you."

Your word against mine. The same threat that Elliott always used again Webb.

If Webb thought it would do any good to beg, he would have been tempted. But a person didn't walk 80 kilometers through remote wilderness to track someone down just to change his mind when the other person pleaded for mercy.

"You took my girlfriend," Brent said. "So I'm going to take away what made her like you. Your music."

Brent put the rifle down and, quick as a snake, grabbed Webb's wrists and yanked him forward onto his belly.

Then Brent stood on Webb's forearms, pinning him in place.

"Let me tell you what I'm going to do," Brent said. "Just 'cause I've had a lot of time to think about how good it will feel to tell you what I'm going to do. I'm going to take away your music by breaking your fingers, one at a time. I'm going to break them so bad, no chance you'll ever be able to play guitar again."

He laughed. "I thought maybe I'd bend your fingers and break them that way, but we've got this pile of rocks here. I'm sure I'll find one the perfect size. It's going to be fun smashing your fingers one by one. All you'll have left inside the skin is little pieces of bone."

Webb squirmed hard, but it was useless. Brent was simply too big.

The pain of Brent's weight on his arms was almost beyond what Webb could bear. He let out a muffled groan at the thought of a rock crushing his fingers.

Then without warning, Brent stepped aside and the pain was gone.

"Don't move," Brent said. Fear filled his voice.

Webb lifted his head. Coming out of the trees, its massive head swinging from side to side, was a grizzly with a white patch of fur just below the shoulders. The one Webb had scared away the day before.

It must have been drawn by the commotion. It paused and stared at them, so close that Webb could smell the bear's intense odor. It smelled like the doorways in the city where homeless men urinated. But way worse.

Webb saw the rifle on the ground. Out of Brent's reach.

Brent dove for the rifle. The sudden movement drew the bear into a charge. With a horrible roar, it lunged forward, jaws open wide.

But Brent was too late. The bear was on both of them.

Webb was blinded by the raking slash of a paw across his face.

Brent screamed.

Webb instinctively pushed backward and over the cliff. Anything to get away from the bear.

Something thumped the back of his head as he fell, and once again, he blacked out.

THIRTY

THEN

In the air-conditioned storage unit, the black-and-white images thrown by the projector had begun with vintage airplanes swooping and looping in a clear sky.

The image had shifted as the camera panned from the sky to the ground, where it focused on a grinning man in a New York Yankees ball cap.

"Talk to us," came the voice of the person holding the camera.

"That's Grandpa Jake," Jana whispered.

"Hey," the man in the cap said into the camera. "I'm Ray Daley, and we're at the 1961 Vintage Air

Show in Las Vegas, Nevada. Above us, David McLean is wowing the crowds in his P-51 Mustang Fighter, showing some of the moves that made him such an amazing pilot when he fought against the Germans only twenty years ago."

The camera zoomed upward again, showing the shiny wings of a plane with a propeller on the nose. A smoke trail showed where it had just done two loops.

Then the camera went back to Ray Daley. His face, of course, was twenty years older than his face in the photo Jana had shown Webb earlier, but he was still recognizable.

"Hello? Jake Rundell?"

A woman's voice came from outside the camera's range. The camera shifted earthward again.

The woman looked like a college girl. Her hair was in a style that Webb remembered from watching Ginger on reruns of *Gilligan's Island.*

"Hello, beautiful!" Ray moved into view, putting his arm on the girl's shoulders and grinning again. "Where you from?"

"Near Nashville, Tennessee," she answered. Her southern drawl was obvious. "A town called Eagleville."

"Come all that ways to see some World War Two pilot heroes, have you?" Ray asked. "Well you don't need to look any further than Jake Rundell and Ray Daley. Stick with us, and we'll show you a good time at the casinos."

"That's exactly why I came all this way," the young woman said, her face serious. "To see the two of you. And David McLean. My name is Ruby Gavin and I—"

"Jake!" Ray shouted and pointed. "Dave's plane. He's in trouble!"

The camera abruptly swung upward to the P-51 Mustang as it did a turning twist, spewing white smoke. The camera stayed on the fighter plane for about ten seconds, long enough to establish that the rolling moves of the plane were part of the show and that there was nothing wrong with the plane.

When the camera swung back to the ground again, Ray Daley was leading the young woman away and had already managed to reach the front row of spectators at the bleachers.

The screen went dark for a moment, but the film reel kept turning. A couple of seconds later, a young girl waved at the camera before jumping off a diving board into a backyard swimming pool.

"That's my mom," Jan said above the clatter of the projector.

The rest of the reel took about eight minutes, and showed nothing more than kids having fun at a swimming pool. Then, without warning, the images stopped, and Webb heard the film flap.

He switched on the lights. The take-up reel was still turning, and the end of the film was making the flapping sound. The empty front reel was spinning but slowing down.

"That's it?" Webb asked.

"Ten minutes," Jana said. "That's all you could get on a reel. Want me to play it again?"

Webb shook his head.

"Time," Webb said, "to open the envelope."

That's where he found a bunch of bank cards, with a yellow sticky note saying the cards held $2,000 in Canadian funds. He also found instructions on how to book flights for the open-ended tickets inside. He was to fly to Norman Wells, in the Northwest Territories, by way of Edmonton, with a stop in Yellowknife.

There were also two more letters. One for him from his grandpa. And one from Jake Rundell to Jim Webb.

THIRTY-ONE

NOW

Webb woke up only because something was pulling hard at the skin of his exposed leg. Something sharp.

He kicked with both legs and heard a scattering of gravel above the sound of rushing water.

It was freezing and his body was convulsing with cold. Much better to go back into the soothing darkness where it was so warm and comfortable. He slipped away.

But then that nipping sensation came again. He growled and kicked, and this time realized that there was an animal on the gravel bank with him.

A wolf. Taking an experimental chew, as if Webb were already dead. The thought horrified him enough to make him roll over and sit up. The wolf backed away and sat on its haunches, staring at Webb.

And a split second later, the reality hit him.

A wolf! Feared predator. Savage beast that hunted in a pack. An animal that could tear out a man's throat.

Webb held his breath. He had an image of the body beneath the pile of rocks, and realized why the rocks had been placed over the body. To keep away animals. Like the wolf.

The wolf panted slightly, tongue hanging out. Webb saw teeth. Big teeth.

What could Webb do to protect himself? He made fists, ready to smack the wolf's nose with his hands bound together. It would be a useless act of defiance, but Webb wasn't going to go down without a fight.

The wolf cocked its head as if it was curious.

Then Webb realized the animal *was* curious, not threatening. Maybe it would sit there for a while. But if it did, would other wolves show up?

Webb lifted his hands and made a shooing motion. "Go!"

The wolf did not go.

But it didn't attack either.

"Heard of *Little Red Riding Hood*?" Webb asked the wolf. He felt silly. But what was he going to do? Jump at the wolf? "It doesn't have a happy ending for you."

The wolf shook its head. It looked like a scornful shake to Webb, but he knew he could be reading too much into the wolf's actions. Webb's entire world right now was his focus on the animal.

The wolf rose and trotted away. If it had just been curious, obviously it had learned what it wanted. But would it return?

Thinking about animals tearing at his flesh made Webb forget about how wet and cold he was. His hands and ankles were still bound with the plastic ties. He had fallen down a cliff and was on a gravel bar in a river in one of the remotest parts of the Arctic, helpless as a newborn.

More images came back to him.

Brent. The rifle. The grizzly.

He had no idea how much time had passed since he fell. Or how far down the river the current had taken him before dumping him on this gravel bar.

Maybe it was a miracle he was alive. He couldn't say, because he had no idea what had actually happened.

He knew, though, that his face hurt where the grizzly had slashed him.

But it wasn't bleeding. He had been unconscious long enough for the blood to start clotting.

Maybe that meant he'd also been unconscious long enough for a search party to start looking for him. Then he remembered. He'd put down a false trail that led north. That's where any searchers would be going. He could yell all he wanted, but nobody was going to hear him.

He'd have to save himself and then hike out.

Something hurt his butt. He shifted, thinking it was a rock, but it was the knife he'd pulled from the skeleton.

Maybe it was a murder weapon, but now it could save Webb's life.

He shifted and squirmed until he managed to slide it out of his pocket. He rolled over, his hands still cuffed, and got to his knees. The knife was on the gravel below him.

His hands were so cold, he could barely hold it.

The blade had rusted a bit, but still had some edge. The rocks must have protected it from water and snow.

He began to saw at the plastic around his ankles. Agonizing minutes later, when the plastic snapped, he yelled with joy.

The next task was more difficult.

He had to sit, squeezing the knife upright between his boots, so that he could saw the plastic around his wrists against it.

It must have been only a matter of minutes, but it seemed like he was sawing for hours. Frustrating as it was, he had no choice. It was either saw through the plastic or become a lifeless piece of meat for the nearby wolf.

Finally there was a snapping sensation. For a second, Webb feared he'd broken the knife blade. But his hands fell loose, and once again he yelled with joy.

He realized, though, that his survival was far from certain.

His entire body was shaking, so much so that he couldn't even hold his hands still.

He needed a fire.

He slapped at his belly. The money belt and matches were still there.

But there wasn't any wood on the gravel bar.

He took a running start and splashed through the river to the shore, discovering how shallow the water was.

That's why he'd lived. The river was running fast, but it wasn't deep. He must have landed on his back in the river, never going under in the current long enough to drown.

On the far bank, he kept moving, tempting as it was to sit down and go to sleep.

He collected small branches and snapped them, grateful that he'd helped George build fires from scratch. Without that, he wouldn't have known what to do, and he didn't have enough matches to learn by making mistakes.

Carefully, he put the small branches down. He prepared larger branches, ready to feed them once the smaller branches caught.

Then he unwrapped his money belt. Safe in the plastic bag were his matches.

He could barely hold them, his fingers were so numb. He managed to get one of the matches to flare, but he was shaking so hard that when he tried to hold it beneath the kindling, the match burned down.

He tried again.

And again.

No way was he going to be able to do it. Why hadn't he thought to put fire starter in the money belt too? George used fire starter; he should have too. Instead, all he had were the bank cards and a few wet receipts from The Northern.

He was going to die, simply because he couldn't hold a match steady enough.

Then Webb grinned.

He'd forgotten about the length of nylon guitar string tucked into his front pocket. String he'd intended to burn at the first opportunity. String that burned just like the wick of a candle.

Looked like the first opportunity would also be the best opportunity.

He used a match to start a small flame at the end of the nylon, and gently slid it into an opening beneath the twigs. The flame wasn't strong, but it was enough.

The first of the twigs caught fire, and then the bigger twigs, and within minutes the fire was strong enough to throw heat.

Webb had always believed that without his J-45, his life would be nothing.

Now he knew it was absolutely true.

THIRTY-TWO

As he rubbed his hands together above the crackling fire, Webb made three assumptions. First of all, he assumed that Brent had not survived the grizzly bear attack. Therefore there was no need to rush to try to find George to mount a rescue mission. While Webb couldn't help thinking about Brent, he did his best not to allow himself to feel much. Dead was horrible enough. Dead by grizzly attack was even worse. But Brent has been ready to smash Webb's fingers and take away Webb's music forever. Webb had tried to help Brent, but the guy had brought his gruesome death upon himself. Should Webb feel terrible for

Brent or glad for himself? He didn't even want to try to come up with an answer.

His second assumption was that if he did not dry his clothes and warm up completely, he might not make it back to the Canol Trail. There was no point in trying to rush; his near-death by hypothermia had weakened him too much to take any risks.

His third assumption was much simpler and beyond argument: since the river had washed him onto the gravel bar, he was downstream of the path that led up to the clifftop and the two bodies. One dead so long that only skeleton and rags remained. The other mangled by a grizzly.

Webb hoped he would recognize the place where he'd fallen down the cliff. All he needed to do was go upstream until he saw it, find the cliff path and follow that path in the other direction, back to the Canol Trail.

Surely the group would be waiting for him at Mile 108 where the chopper was supposed to pick them up.

But what if they weren't? What if the chopper had arrived and taken them away? No one knew where he'd gone. To them it would have been like he'd simply disappeared.

But no, wouldn't they look for him?

Except where would they start looking?

Thinking about that made him uneasy, and he started to second-guess whether he should spend an hour or two in front of the fire to get completely dry.

He was beginning to feel stronger, wasn't he?

He rubbed his hands again, looking at his fingers as if seeing them for the first time. He shuddered, wondering what it would have been like if Brent had crushed them slowly with the rocks.

It made him think of the knife that had saved his life, the knife he'd pulled from the ribs of a skeleton. Had it been someone working the Canol Trail all those years ago? But how could his grandpa have known about it? Webb had heard a lot of stories about his grandpa's travels, but not one that put him here in the Northwest Territories. Had his grandpa been here once and kept it a secret from the family?

He looked more closely at the knife.

And saw three initials. *DAM.*

David Adam McLean.

His grandfather.

THIRTY-THREE

Webb knew where he was, even if no one else did. It was a simple matter of making it back to the Canol Trail and then seeing if George was anywhere nearby.

It took him twenty minutes to fight his way back over those couple of hundred meters, twenty minutes of ducking branches, stepping in soggy soil, splashing through water, squeezing between bushes. Twenty minutes of thinking about how each step took him closer to the spot where a grizzly bear might still be crouched over Brent's body.

He couldn't escape the thought of the grizzly protecting its kill from scavengers. Or returning to it every few hours. The closer he got to the spot, the closer he was to the grizzly.

When he saw the path that went up to the clifftop, all he wanted to do was make a dash in the direction of the Canol Trail, just in case the grizzly was up there and had heard him crashing through the underbrush.

But there was this nagging doubt that he couldn't push aside.

What if Brent wasn't dead? Webb was only a few minutes away from the top of the cliff. What if Webb was walking away from a man he could rescue by taking those few minutes to see if Brent was alive?

Webb stood at the base of the cliff, head craned upward, trying to hear any kind of sound that would let him know if the grizzly was still up there. It was impossible to hear anything above the roar of the river.

When he made his decision, it was because he imagined a conversation with his grandfather.

"Webby, if you walk away from this, for the rest of your life you'll wonder if you left someone to die. Is that something you want to take with you to your grave?"

"*Compared to you knowing you killed a man and buried him with your knife still in his ribs—didn't you take that with you to your grave?*"

"*It's not about me, Webby. I am in my grave. What's done is done. It's about you now. How will you feel if you leave him scared and alone, getting weaker and weaker?*"

Webb shook his head.

His grandfather would have been right.

Webb threw away his first assumption that Brent was dead, and slowly and carefully began to climb again.

Brent was a crumpled and bloody mess near the pile of stones that hid the skeleton. The rifle was on the ground beside Brent's broken body.

But there was no sign of the grizzly.

His own terrified breath rasping, Webb advanced to Brent and knelt beside him. It was difficult to take in how much damage the grizzly had done. Webb fought the impulse to puke.

Then he saw something he could barely believe: the slightest movement in the soft part of Brent's exposed throat.

"You alive?" Webb whispered, leaning in.

Brent opened an eye. The white of his eye was a startling contrast to the bloody red of his face.

Brent groaned. "It's back."

Webb's skin prickled. He put his hand on the rifle. He heard that horrible roar again and spun around.

Ten paces away, the grizzly was swaying its head back and forth. Sniffing.

Webb knew that while a grizzly didn't have vision as sharp as an eagle or fox, it certainly wasn't blind. The grizzly would easily see movement. He realized the wind was blowing from the grizzly toward him. Grizzlies have such a keen sense of smell, even with the wind in the wrong direction, any second it might pick up his scent.

Webb commanded himself to keep calm. The rifle was in his hand, but if he lifted it and then tried to check the safety, the grizzly would be on him in a flash.

Staring at the grizzly, holding his breath, Webb felt along the rifle until his fingers hit the safety. He glanced down. The safety was still on.

He clicked it off.

That slight sound was all it took.

The grizzly roared and lunged again, so close now that Webb saw saliva spraying from its jaws.

On his knees, Webb lifted and fired. Once. He tried again, but the trigger didn't move. Not enough time to hit the pump action and reload, as George had taught him.

Webb knew he was dead.

Still on his knees, all he could do was jam the butt of the rifle into the ground and cower beneath it. It was about as much protection as an umbrella.

The grizzly fell, its full weight on the tip of rifle, landing on it like it was a spear.

Webb rolled to one side as a huge paw slammed down and hit his shoulder. But that was it. Nothing else. No mauling, no slashing. No jaws snapping shut on his skull. Just an overwhelming stench.

The bear was silent.

As the rifle toppled sideways, so did the grizzly.

Dead.

Huddled in a ball, Webb only managed to say one word. "Crap."

He stood up and saw part of the grizzly's chest torn open.

One bullet. One very lucky bullet. He'd hit the grizzly with his first and only shot, and even as it died, the bear's momentum and power had almost been enough to kill Webb.

Beside him, Brent groaned again. "Water."

Webb struggled to focus on the situation.

Brent needed immediate medical help. No way could Webb carry him. That meant he'd have to bring the others to this spot.

They'd find another body buried under a rock pile and ask too many questions about it. They'd ask him what had led him there. They'd try to identify the body, and sooner or later they'd link Webb to his grandfather and learn that his grandfather had sent him here, and then they'd reach the obvious conclusion. At some point David McLean had been in the Northwest Territories, and at some point David McLean had put a knife into the ribs of a man and buried him just off the Canol Trail. There could be no other reason David McLean had not once mentioned the Northwest Territories in all his travel stories. The entire world would know that his grandfather was a murderer.

Then why had his grandfather gone to all the trouble to send Webb to this spot?

Each of these requests, these tasks, his grandfather had said from beyond the grave, *has been specifically selected for you to fulfill. All of the things you will need to complete your task will be provided—money, tickets, guides—everything…It is so sad that I will not be there to watch you all grow into the incredible men I know you will be. But I don't need to be there to know that will happen. I am so certain of that. As certain as I am that I will be there with you as you complete my last requests, as you continue your life journeys.*

Remembering those words, Webb felt like his grandfather was right beside him. If Webb was to grow into an incredible man, then Webb couldn't make the journey by hiding a secret like this.

Webb had always trusted his grandfather. He wasn't going to stop now.

Webb took the rifle and pointed it at the sky. He cocked and fired it, the thunder of the shot reverberating around him. He cocked and fired again. Then a third time.

Three shots. The universal signal for help.

Webb set down the rifle. He took off his jacket and used it to make a pillow beneath Brent's head.

Then Webb headed down the path to the river.

Brent needed water. Webb would get it by soaking his shirt in the river and squeezing the water into Brent's mouth.

Webb gave a tight smile. He was doing this because Brent was alive. As for the other long-dead body and his grandfather's long-buried secret?

Let the dead take care of the dead.

PART
THREE

MONSTERS

Under the bed
What's in my head
That I can't see
You walk the halls
I hear your steps
You haunt my dreams

You're running for me
You're running for me
I'm coming for you
You're running for me
You're running for me
I'm coming for you

Monsters
Taking out Monsters
One by one
Two by two
Turn the tables on you
Taking out my Monsters tonight

Here on my skin
The fathers' sins
Leave a scar
That you can trace
Can you erase
The devil's mark

Nowhere to hide
Won't let you hide
Drag you into the light
Not afraid to fight
This is do or die
Say your prayers tonight

Monsters
Taking out Monsters
One by one
Two by two
Turn the tables on you
Taking out my Monsters tonight

THIRTY-FOUR

NOW

Webb jumped out of the back of a pickup truck with his guitar case strapped to his back, and gave a big thumbs-up to the farmer who had given him a ride down the highway.

The old farmer gave a slight dignified nod, and left Webb at the only traffic light in the town of Eagleville, Tennessee.

Five days had passed since he'd been at Devil's Pass. When Webb had flown out of Toronto the day before, it had been a soggy, chilly day, wet leaves falling to the ground and sticking, unmoved by gusts of wind.

In Tennessee, the sky was cloudless and the air pressed warmth upon him.

Webb took in his surroundings, thinking of the beautiful, harsh desolation of the Northwest Arctic and comparing it to the comfort of the old buildings around him.

There was a post office across the street. And a town hall, built with logs, with rocking chairs on the front porch. More importantly, there was a cafe called the Main Street Cafe, right beside a barbershop.

Webb was hungry.

He stepped inside, and the smile on the face of the waitress was as warm as the air outside. "Honey, git you a tea?"

"I'd like something a little cooler than that," Webb said. "I'm thirsty."

She stared at him, puzzled for a moment, Then grinned. "Honey, I kin tell you ain't from around here. Minnesota?"

"Canada."

"Same thing, honey," she said. "Any tea you git here is nice and cool. You want hot tea, you have to order hot tea."

"Thanks," Webb said. He looked at the menu. It said *Meat and three.*

"Meat and three what?" he asked.

"You order a meat, honey. Then you get your choice of three sides."

She pointed to the menu. "See there. Grits, maybe. Okra. But I'll tell you what. That creamed corn? Today people bin telling me it's like the cook put his foot in it."

"Probably won't order it then," Webb said.

She laughed. "That means he done a good job. Gave it everything he got. If you haven't eaten at a meat and three, I'd go with pulled pork, then creamed corn, sweet potato pie and taters."

"Sure," Webb said. On his return to Toronto from Devil's Pass, Webb had called the lawyer, John Devine, to report what had happened. Webb had learned from Devine that he was to make his way to Eagleville, a small town south and east of Nashville.

"Honey," the waitress said, pointing at the guitar, "you planning on making it big here?"

"I just travel with it," Webb said, thinking the waitress would never believe where the Gibson had been a few days earlier. "Maybe you can help me. I'm looking for Ruby Gavin."

"You kin?"

"I'm glad I can," Webb said. "Thanks. Just need directions."

More laughter from the waitress. "What I mean is, are you Ruby's kin? Kinfolk?"

"Just delivering something," Webb said.

THIRTY-FIVE

Ruby's small white house was only a couple of blocks down the road from the Main Street Cafe.

She lived near the Eagleville United Methodist Church. The paint on the house was faded, and vines crawled up the railing of the front porch. A woman Webb assumed was Ruby was sitting in a rocking chair, waving at him.

"Honey, you look just like how Shirley described you," Ruby said. "Was the pulled pork any good today?"

Webb nodded, not surprised that the waitress had called ahead, given that Eagleville only had one traffic light and, so far, everybody called him honey.

As he got closer, he saw fine wrinkles all across Ruby's face. She had to be well over seventy. She was a slight woman, wearing a long dress with a pattern of pink flowers on it. A set of wire-rimmed glasses sat at the tip of her nose. She had a pitcher of iced tea on a table beside her and some glasses.

There was also a white and orange FedEx package beside her.

"Jim Webb?" she asked. "I've been expecting you."

"It was the waitress at the Main Street, right?"

"She did call," Ruby admitted. "But this morning I received another phone call. From a lawyer fellow up in Canada named Devine. Said I'd be getting a FedEx package and asked if I'd give it to a long-haired kid named Jim Webb when he showed up later today."

She tapped the box. "It's all yours."

She laughed. "First FedEx I've ever had delivered here, and turned out it was for someone else. Life's funny, isn't it?"

Webb nodded.

"And," she said, "life's curious. I've been sitting here all day, wondering why someone I don't know would show up from Canada to collect a FedEx, when I see on the label that it came from the same place you just left."

"Well," Webb said, "I don't have an explanation for the FedEx. But I do have a reason for visiting."

Webb was nervous. He'd been thinking this through for a while, wondering how it might go, wondering how to start. So he sat down and told her about walking the Canol Trail, about the grizzly, and about Brent. How a helicopter had airlifted Brent back to Norman Wells, and how he'd been in serious condition but ended up making it just fine, except for the hundreds of stitches it had taken to pull him together.

She leaned in and soaked up every word as he told her his tale, but when he finished he still hadn't told her the most important part.

Webb tried a few times and couldn't find a way to say it.

Finally she said, "It's fine. Just say what you need to say."

What came out then, despite all his rehearsing, was only a few words. "I found something that might mean a lot to you."

He set the small ceramic pendant on the table. And the military dog tag with the name Harlowe Gavin.

She leaned forward. She ignored the dog tag and peered at the ceramic pendant for a few moments, then sat back.

Webb wondered if he needed to tell her what it was, but then he saw tears filling her eyes.

"Oh, Lord," she finally said in a near whisper. Then she was quiet for a while.

She drew a deep breath, as if she was pulling in strength, and turned to Webb. "Every day since I was eight years old, I've thought about that heart. Every day. I made it for him in school. Smoothed out the clay. I can still smell it, you know. It was damp and covered in cloth and the teacher used a cheese cutter to slice off a piece and handed it to me."

Webb didn't know how clay smelled when it was damp, but he nodded.

"I wanted it to be perfect. For Father's Day. I used a knife to cut the heart shape, and the end of a wire to draw in my initials on one side, and *I love you forever, Daddy* on the other side. Then I painted it with colored glazes, and my teacher put it in the kiln. When it came out, I knew that it was going to last forever too. I gave it to my daddy, and he was so proud of it, he bought a gold chain and strung it around his neck. I was proud too, seeing him in a uniform, knowing he had the necklace underneath it. He was a pilot in the war and then he was sent north to help with an army project, and he never came back. I never stopped hoping I'd see him walk down the street toward our house."

She was quiet for a while, lost in memory.

Webb knew better than to break the silence.

"Folks said he deserted the air force," she said. "Said maybe he found another woman. They can be cruel like that, you know, thinking it won't reach a little girl's ears. But I never believed it. Not my daddy."

She turned on Webb, suddenly fierce. "He wouldn't run away on me. And don't you tell me different."

Webb shook his head. "I won't. Someone killed him."

"Oh, Lord," she said again. Then she wept openly. When she regained her composure, she said, "I can die happy now I know my daddy didn't run away on me."

Then she leaned forward, intensity glittering in her eyes. "Tell me who murdered my daddy."

THIRTY-SIX

"My grandfather, David McLean, was a pilot in the same squadron as your father," Webb began. "There were four of them, good friends. You probably have the same photo as Jake Rundell."

"Jake Rundell," she said. "David McLean. Ray Daley. And my daddy."

"You went to an air show in Las Vegas," Webb said. "You wanted to ask my grandfather and Jake Rundell and Ray Daley if they knew anything at all about your father."

"I did," she said. "Ray Daley spent hours with me, talking about my father. He promised he'd do what he could. But I never heard from him."

Webb remembered the young woman on the movie screen in Arizona. Then, as now, there was a sadness in her eyes that was impossible to miss.

"Ray Daley loved to gamble," Webb said. All of what he was about to tell Ruby had been waiting for him in a letter at the lawyer's office on his return from Norman Wells. "He wasn't good at it. Trouble was, he had a habit of pretending his name was Harlowe Gavin. They looked a lot alike, and he'd gotten away with it many times. Your father and Ray were sent to the Arctic to fly in and out of Alaska during the building of the Canol Road, and Ray kept gambling at the work camps, using your father's name. He gambled with the wrong set of men, and they paid someone in the camp to make an example of Ray. Except the person they sent went to the real Harlowe Gavin, took him up the trail, away from one of the work sites, and—"

Webb couldn't say the words.

"Took my daddy's life," Ruby Gavin finished for him.

"With his own knife, a knife my grandfather had given him when their air force careers took them on different paths."

When Webb thought of the lonely pile of rocks and of a man buried there for sixty years and the little girl waiting for her daddy to come home to this small town, he had to turn his head and blink away tears before continuing.

"Ray knew they'd kill him next if they found out what happened. He took your father's paycheck too, and signed up for a flight to Whitehorse, pretending to be your dad. The work camp had thousands of military and thousands of workers, and it was easy to take advantage of the confusion. He cashed in the paycheck and bought a train ticket under your father's name, and made sure people knew he got on the train. He jumped off just as it was leaving, and made his way back to the camp. And when the army went looking for your father, they tracked down where the paycheck had been cashed."

"But you weren't born for fifty years after that," Ruby said. "You show up out of nowhere and tell me this. I want to believe it so badly. But I don't know who you are."

"A good man's grandson. Ray Daley lived with his secret for a long time, but in the end, he had to tell someone before he died. A few months back, on his deathbed, he made a phone call to Jake Rundell and confessed."

"I should have heard about it from Jake then," she said. "Not you."

"Jake didn't want to believe Ray. The four of them had all been so close. Ray was old and not everything he said made sense."

"Alzheimer's?" Ruby Gavin asked.

Webb nodded. "Jake wasn't going to go to the authorities and damage Ray's reputation unless he was convinced it had happened the way Ray said it had. He called my grandfather for advice. They decided to send someone for proof. Me."

"You. All the way to the Arctic?"

"My grandfather had his reasons."

"I'd like to thank your grandfather," Ruby said.

"He was the kind of guy who didn't need thanks," Webb said.

"Didn't?"

"I miss him," Webb said. He wanted to go now. He couldn't bear the sorrow he was feeling for this woman. He couldn't bear his own sorrow. He stood.

"I expect you'll hear something official from the police," Webb said. "My grandfather's lawyer, he made an arrangement. He wasn't going to release any information to the police until I had a chance to come down here first and tell you myself."

"Makes me want to start dancing," Ruby said. "I'm calling everyone I know. Harlowe Gavin didn't run out on his family."

She pointed at the Methodist church. "We're going to have his funeral right there. If you're not shy with that guitar, maybe you can play a song for him."

Webb was about to say he'd be gone by then, but he made the mistake of looking directly at Ruby and seeing a little girl instead of an old woman.

"Sure," Webb said. "I might have a song or two for him."

THIRTY-SEVEN

Back at the Main Street Cafe and armed with coffee and a cinnamon bun the size of a loaf of bread, Webb opened the FedEx package.

He slid the contents onto the table. There was a note on Devine's stationery, an envelope with his grandfather's handwriting on the outside and a thin legal-sized folder. The note had simple instructions: *Read your grandfather's letter before looking inside the folder.*

Webb shook his head and grinned in admiration at his grandfather. He'd been larger than life in life, and now, even in death, he still managed to be as large as possible.

Webb took a bite out of the cinnamon bun and a sip of coffee. He suspected this was going to be the last letter from Grandpa. He was in no hurry to read it, because then all of it would be over.

Another bite of cinnamon bun, and another sip of coffee. Finally, he opened the envelope from his grandpa and pulled out the letter.

First things first, Webby. I've been saving a surprise for you. I've paid for you to have a week's worth of studio time in Nashville with a great producer. Get some of your songs on iTunes, okay? I know you've got the talent, and more importantly, I know you want it bad enough to achieve your dreams in the music world. When the songs get out there, I know the world's going to come calling for you.

Second thing: Webby, if you are reading this in Devine's office, it means that you found nothing in the Arctic, and that poor Ray Daley was a delusional old man.

But if you're reading this after talking to Ruby Gavin, that means you found the remains of her father. I didn't want you to get this letter and the folder until you learned the price she had to pay for the secret that was buried for so long.

Webby, secrets are such a heavy burden; they can destroy lives. Ray was never the same after the war, and if you are in Tennessee as you read this, now we know why. The secret was destroying him too.

What about your secret, Webby?

It worried me greatly, watching you change in the years after your mother married Elliott Skinner. You were once so open and affectionate and joyful, like that beagle of yours. Nibbles? Or maybe it was Niblet.

Slowly you became tougher and colder. I'd ask your mother about it, but Charlotte always kept a bright face, said things were great at home.

Let me ask you this, Webby. Who sent the letter to your principal telling her to look in your locker for marijuana? Don't be surprised I know about this. I've been worried about you for years, and I've tried to let very little escape me when it comes to your life.

Here's my guess. I think you sent the letter. I think you were looking for the perfect excuse to get out of the house without forcing your mother to wonder if the real reason was Elliott.

Remember that day you asked me to co-sign a loan for a J-45? It got me to wondering why you'd need another guitar, because I knew nothing was more important to you than the guitar your dad left you when he died. That's when I decided I would do what I could to find out about Elliott.

I went to your mother, and she said Elliott never hurt her or hurt you. When I said I didn't believe her, she admitted that she always felt afraid around him, even though she couldn't explain it in a way that didn't make her sound crazy, and that it was slowly making her feel smaller and smaller. She said it broke her heart when you left the house after telling Elliott you never wanted to talk to her again. But at the same time, she felt that somehow it was safer for you not to be living at home.

Webby, that's not how people should live. In fear.

The folder should help. Read it, and then let Devine advise you on the best way to use what's in the folder. Do it on your terms. Not Elliott's.

Webb wanted to throw his coffee mug through the front window of the restaurant. He hadn't told Elliott he never wanted to talk to his mother again. Elliott had made sure Webb stayed away from her and then lied about it.

He fought the rage, and finally, he slowly and calmly put the letter back into the envelope.

It was the only way to control himself, because if he gave in to his emotions in the slightest, the dam would break and he'd go berserk right there in the Main Street Cafe.

His growing feeling of cold rage told Webb that his grandfather was right. He was becoming Elliott. He had wanted to run over Brent in Norman Wells, he'd wanted to smash Fritz in the head with a rock. Normal humans don't respond like that.

Webb forced himself to sip his coffee until the feeling subsided.

Then he opened the folder. It contained two pages. The first page was a letter from a private investigation firm, stating that the summary that followed was based on factual evidence that could be backed up in court.

The second page was the summary of the investigation into the events that led to the dishonorable discharge of Elliott McLuhan Skinner from the Canadian Armed Forces.

Dishonorable?

But Elliott Skinner had presented himself as a soldier honorably discharged, and built up his security firm on that reputation.

Webb read the second page three times. Phrases had been highlighted.*Dishonorable discharge based on overly harsh discipline with recruits. Anger management issues with inappropriate responses to anyone who challenged his authority. Dishonorable discharge hidden by altered computer records and false references. Confirmed assessment as a borderline psychopath, according to the PCL-R testing standards.*

Webb didn't care what PCL-R stood for, but felt an amazing relief that the secret didn't need to remain hidden. That someone else—someone who would be believed—could confirm what had been happening. Webb closed the folder and stared at it so long that the waitress came over and asked if anything was the matter.

Webb told her no.

He put the note and the letter from his grandfather and the folder from the private investigator back into the FedEx package and put the package into his guitar case.

He stepped outside into the heat. He sat on a bench on the sidewalk and looked at the sky as if he could peer into heaven and see his grandfather.

Then he took out his phone and dialed a number that he had not dialed in a long, long time.

When the person on the other end answered, he began to cry.

"Mom," he said. "I want to come home."

ACKNOWLEDGMENTS

Many thanks to Eric Walters for giving me the chance to be involved in this great project. Thanks also to editor Sarah Harvey for providing encouragement and insight and to Andrew Wooldridge and everyone else at Orca. It's so fun and rewarding to work with the team. And thank you to Canadian North airlines for all their help with my travels to the North and their support for literacy for the students in the Northwest Arctic. Thanks as well to Drew Ramsey and Ram Bam Thank You Ma'am, BMI, for production of the song "Monsters," which can be heard at www.seventheseries.com or on iTunes.

SIGMUND BROUWER is the bestselling author of books for both children and adults, including *Rock & Roll Literacy* and titles in the Orca Echoes, Orca Currents and Orca Sports series. Visit www.rockandroll-literacy.com for more information about Sigmund's presentations. Sigmund and his family divide their time between Eagleville, Tennessee, and Red Deer, Alberta.

THE SEVEN SERIES

SEVEN
SERIES

7 GRANDSONS
7 JOURNEYS
7 AUTHORS
1 AMAZING SERIES

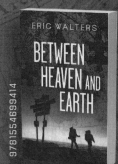

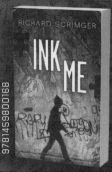